Emily Lickenson's The Case of Dead Words

CEECEE JAMES

Copyright © 2024 by CeeCee James

All rights reserved.

No part of this book may be reproduced in any form or by any electronic or mechanical means, including information storage and retrieval systems, without written permission from the author, except for the use of brief quotations in a book review.

Cover by Pixel Squirrel

For my Family

Contents

Untitled   vii

Chapter 1   1
Chapter 2   9
Chapter 3   19
Chapter 4   29
Chapter 5   37
Chapter 6   43
Chapter 7   49
Chapter 8   61
Chapter 9   69
Chapter 10   73
Chapter 11   79
Chapter 12   85
Chapter 13   91
Chapter 14   95
Chapter 15   101
Chapter 16   109
Chapter 17   119
Chapter 18   125
Chapter 19   129
Chapter 20   135
Chapter 21   141
Chapter 22   151

Afterword   157

Untitled

I'm excited to share a new series! Book one, The Route 66 Misfits, starring Clara Fitzwater from the Secret Library Cozy Mystery series!

The famed Clara Fitzwater is now is trading her stage lights for detective work. Traveling in her restore ancient Volkswagen van, adorned with sun-bleached daisies and peace signs, she's living life just the way she wanted.

Until, late one night, she gets an urgent call from her niece, Jane, who's not just been mugged but is also upstaging the local drama scene with her unexpected starring role as the prime suspect.

With Jane's future hanging by a thread thinner than the script she's writing in jail, Clara and her actor friend, Archie, dive into the investigation. Archie, sit-com extraordinaire, is more used to delivering punchlines than solving crimes. But he brings his comedic timing to the case, much to Clara's chagrin. Together, they navigate through the mystery to find who framed Jane.

Will Clara's theatrical flair and Archie's knack for improvisation be enough to unravel this mystery? Or will their curtain call come too soon, leaving Jane to face the final act alone?

Chapter One

Have you ever experienced one of those mornings where everything about your bed feels absolutely perfect? The warmth is just right, your toes are snug under the blankets, and you've nestled perfectly into your pillow. You feel like you could stay there, perhaps even forever.

But then, the phone rings.

Yes, it was one of those kinds of mornings for me.

"Hello?" I let my voice be extra sleepy so whoever was on the other end would feel guilty. She didn't, because it was my Aunt Mattie. She never felt guilty about anything she did. It was a power she had to disregard people's feelings just to right the wrong. I wanted to be just like her — but I had such a long way to go to get there.

"Emily?" Aunt Mattie squawked, sounding mortified to find me still asleep.

"Good morning. I was just getting up," I lied, knowing I would probably get a lecture regardless. I was right.

"Don't tell me that, my girl. I can practically hear the wisps of dreams leaving in your voice."

"I'm up. I'm up."

"You know what they say about the early bird and the worm."

"And you know what I say back about early worms. Those poor things should have slept in."

She snorted. "Well, that's true, I suppose. We don't like the worms, at least not to eat. But they are good for the garden." Her voice dropped as she thought. "What on earth is that little rhyme about anyway? You're right. It makes no sense. However, the point is, getting up earlier helps get things done. Why, just look at me. I've been up since six this morning," Her voice acquired the tone that let me know the lecture was still about to roll out.

"Yes, I know, Aunt Mattie."

Too late. She launched off into her story.

I glanced over at the clock and groaned inwardly. Shakespeare, my cat and best friend, leaped onto the foot of the bed, running his heavy weight along the length of my leg. Of course, I knew what he wanted. He was hungry. He was always hungry. He took after my aunt, however. Demanding. Once, he waited until I was ensconced in bed, nearly ready to doze off, and then he jumped on my face to let me know his cat food bowl was only half-way full.

Cats. Oh, there was no denying that I loved Shakespeare. That was his name. In fact, my whole job centered around cats, since my job was to blog for the Whiskers Food company.

Aunt Mattie still rattled on in an animated tone. I thought perhaps I should listen. "Exercise. Exercise is what you need, my girl," she was saying.

I had to admit that exercise was the last thing I had in mind. "Yeah, I totally agree."

I was trying to craft a way to gently end the call when she delivered her punchline, "I'm so glad to hear you say that, because, I've signed us up for yoga at the community center. We start today!"

Shocked, I nearly dropped the phone. "Yoga? Today?" I stammered, the perfect morning now a distant memory as the reality of bending and stretching set in.

"Yes, today!" she confirmed with enthusiasm. "And don't you try to wiggle out of it. It'll be good for us. Besides, I've already told everyone you're an expert. You can show them your moves!"

I bit back a laugh, knowing that my expertise was limited to stretching to reach the remote. "Aunt Mattie, I've never done yoga in my life."

"Perfect!" she exclaimed, missing the point entirely. "You'll be a natural then. See you at eight. Don't be late!"

The line clicked off. I stared at Shakespeare, who now sat by his bowl with a look of feline amusement. "Don't you start," I warned him, but he just flicked his tail, clearly enjoying my predicament.

Resigned, I swung my legs out of bed. The cold floor sent a shiver up my spine, a stark contrast to the warmth I had just abandoned. As I prepared to face the day, and the yoga mat, I couldn't help but shake my head at Aunt Mattie's boundless energy and her knack for pulling me into her schemes.

I glanced at my cat. "Well, buddy, looks like we're doing yoga. Let's hope I can at least touch my toes."

As I shuffled towards the kitchen, my mind started spinning with ideas for my next blog post: "The Zen of Cat Food – How Yoga Can Improve Your Cat's Life."

I shook out the food and gave his head a scratch.

Maybe Aunt Mattie was onto something after all. Maybe this would be a new adventure, or at least, a new source of comedy for my readers. And perhaps, just maybe, I'd learn to appreciate the early worm... or at least understand why it should've stayed in bed.

Shakespeare wrapped himself around my ankles to thank me for his meal. After another quick pat, I ran to the bathroom. A quick brush through my hair and a rub under my eyes to catch the leftover mascara, then on to my closet.

Just in time. Aunt Mattie was ringing the bell from the street level exactly fifteen minutes early. I slung my lightest purse over my shoulder on its thin strap. I had no idea what this yoga would look like, but I did know she was fond of stopping for tea and cookies. She always tried to pay, but I liked to do my fair share.

Now impatient knocks came at the door. "Are you awake? Yoohoo!"

Quickly, I opened the door. "You're early."

"Best habit ever. You ready to go?"

"Yes, am I dressed appropriately?"

She glanced me over, her painted eyebrows scrunching. "Bad news. It turns out I had the wrong day. Yoga starts tomorrow."

I blinked at her. "Are you serious?"

"Yes, so instead I've decided we're going for a walk. Exercise, girl, and I like to explore a bit. I have to admit, it's getting boring looking out the same window every day. Let's take a look around your neighborhood."

"You want to go for a walk?" I glanced at her leg that had only recently recovered from injury.

"Don't be a ninny, my leg is fine." She looked over my shoulder. "And it looks like that cat wants to go as well."

Shakespeare gave a resounding yowl, showing his canine teeth. It did indeed sound like he wanted to join us for a morning jaunt and didn't want me to be a ninny, as well. I gave up and found his harness. After a quick buckle of the clasp, I had him in it.

"All right, let's go," I said, winding up the leash.

I took the stairs downward with practiced strides. She followed right along next to me.

"You're in a hurry," she announced loudly so that the entire world could hear.

I slowed to a stop. "I'm sorry, going too fast? I knew we should watch your leg. Maybe we should skip the walk."

"My goodness. Someone woke up on the wrong side of the bed," she said, adjusting the glasses she wore around her neck.

"Someone woke me up, that's for sure," I reminded, setting down my cat.

"Well, Mr. Shakespeare wants a walk. I'm not one to deny a cat."

Shakespeare rubbed against her leg. He liked the feel of her stockings. Without a glance at me, she rustled in her purse and pulled out a small green bag with a cat on it. She shook out a treat and bent down to give it to him.

The pupils of his eyes widened as he delicately smelled it. He took it, and she scratched behind his ears. She caught me watching. "What, my girl? Someone has to feed him. Poor boy is starving."

His belly nearly hung to the ground, so that wasn't true. But we were working on that. Hence the walk.

"So, which way do you want to go?" I glanced left down the street and then back at her. She had already turned and was heading east with a decidedly purposeful step. She wheeled around and waved her thin hand.

"You know, I don't believe I've ever been down that street," she said as she pointed toward an older part of town where factories had come and gone over the years. "It looks fascinating. Let's have a peek."

"I think that might not be a good idea," I warned, inwardly cringing. The sun was barely over the tops of the buildings. "I'm told that's a pretty rough neighborhood."

"Oh, psh. I'm not afraid of a few rowdy teenagers." She continued on with determined steps.

I rolled my eyes and felt my pocket to make sure I had my phone. For someone who was good at giving orders, she was lousy at taking advice.

"Come on, darling," she called back. "Don't dawdle. The day will come when you will be glad that you can walk." She continued down the sidewalk.

Shakespeare tugged at the slender leash that was anchored to his collar. Even Shakespeare seemed to understand that Aunt Mattie was in charge of the outing.

And so our adventure began.

Chapter Two

Aunt Mattie continued north, toward the rougher, industrial side of town. I seldom had business in that part of town, and I had to admit, it was interesting. After all, it was still early morning. I presumed that all those who tended to skulk and commit crimes understood the area was off-limits until at least ten p.m.

This part of the neighborhood was called Shoetown, known for the hundred-year-old shoe factory that had once provided the town's primary source of jobs. As we walked closer, a dismal, four-story building loomed in front of us.

"My goodness, what a sight," Aunt Mattie said.

"You remember it being in operation?" I asked.

"Ages ago. When I was a girl, my brother and I used to explore here." Her eyes softened at the memory. "Let's go have a look."

Across from the factory was an empty lot. Something had been bulldozed there and never rebuilt.

I could understand why they hadn't. Despite Aunt Mattie's warm memories, Shoetown was quite a sight, and not in a let's build a business next to it type of way. With its broken windows, expected brick decay, and boarded-up doors, it pretty much screamed "Keep away." There was an alley leading to a loading area at its back.

Aunt Mattie bent forward, stretching her neck to look down the alley. She then nodded. "Forward ho!" she shouted as if we were part of a wagon train.

"No way, Aunt Mattie. I'm not going down there, and neither are you. There's nothing down there that needs seeing that badly."

"All of us neighbor kids used to play back there years ago. Come along now, my girl. Where's your gumption? Our family line is known for it."

"Nope. I'm putting my foot down on this occasion. Let's get back, and I'll make you some breakfast. Besides, I have work to do."

"Work? What work?"

"Why do you always tease me about being a blogger for the Whisker Treats Cat Food Company? You know I have to get my articles in to make my rent."

"I always told you I can help you out so you don't have to work. Besides, if a cat needs to be fed, it catches a mouse, or even a rat," she finished, glancing to the left as a rodent ran under a dumpster.

I shivered. "Please, let's go. And I don't want Shakespeare to be eating a rat! The very idea freaks me out!"

"Fine, I won't say another word." She paused to consider me over her glasses. "But I wish you'd reconsider my offer."

"Thank you anyway. That's so kind, but I like working."

She stopped and looked at me, her head tipped downward as her eyebrows became lines over her thin nose. I knew that look.

"I do!" I insisted. "I promise."

"Very well. But look! Shakespeare is curious."

"It's the rodent," I said. He did seem interested. Then again, maybe the comment about rats had him intrigued.

"Come on, let's just take a quick peek. It's an adventure! The sun is shining. The birds are chirping. I just want to see if they left the wishing tree. I left a penny in it once."

Wishing tree? I tried to convince myself it was an adventure. Besides, by her expression, I knew if I'd refused to go, she very well could go on her own.

Her ability to convince people amazed me. I'd seen her do it with police officers, detectives, even ministers who were sworn to oaths. She just started down this meandering path of words, asking them questions in six different ways, and soon they were so frustrated that they revealed exactly what she wanted to know. I found it to be one of her more charming qualities, however, it was less charming when directed at me.

"Whoops! There he goes!" Aunt Mattie said.

I glanced down to see Shakespeare had wiggled out of his harness. "Shakespeare!" I yelled. And darn it if he didn't run right toward that dumpster where we'd seen the rodent.

"Let's go get him!" she called and was hurrying after him.

I was a little surprised in that she had walked as far as she had. In the recent past, she had suffered an injury to her leg, and I thought she should still be careful. The entire affair had put her into a nursing home where she probably solved the murder of another resident.

She seemed to attract them — like ants to a drop of spilled honey. Crime seemed to find her, particularly murderers.

While Aunt Mattie was perched on a short concrete support wall, and Shakespeare happily sniffing in and out of every dark hole and crevice he could find, I was deep in my musings and ignoring the fact that we were standing in a very dangerous area of town. I was being lured off guard. That was when it happened.

I caught a movement from the corner of my eye and then was attacked. It was Shakespeare. He had flown upward onto my leg, his claws digging into my pants.

"What is it? Shakespeare? What's wrong?"

"What's that cat got into now?" Aunt Mattie wanted to know.

"I don't know. This is unlike him."

She clucked her tongue. "I told you he was interested down here."

"You know, there is a coincidence here. Every time Shakespeare finds something to become alarmed about, you happen to be with us. Now why do you suppose that is?"

"Not the last time," she pointed out, saucily.

"No, not at the very beginning, but you quickly immerse yourself into the whole thing."

"Are you saying you'd like me to stay out of your business?"

"Oh, could the heavens be so kind?"

"Don't be impertinent, my girl. You forget. Without me, you would have no solution."

"And you, dear aunt, forget that without me, neither would you."

I was conducting this conversation quite calmly, given the fact that a cat had attached itself to my pants and was wildly trying to climb. But when I tried to pick him up, he kicked away and jumped back to the ground.

"Shakespeare, you know better than that." I grabbed for the leash.

Instead of being a good cat and listening to me, he skittered down an alley between two buildings. There was nothing left for me to do but to follow.

"Where are you going?"

"It's Shakespeare. He's leading me somewhere."

"And you think that it's me that attracts crimes?"

"Who brought us here in the first place?"

That's when I froze. Was it possible that someone was lurking down the alley, waiting for us? Would they try to jump me, perhaps steal my bag or even... worse?

Shakespeare leaped onto the dumpster, and before I could grab him, horror of horrors, he stretched up to a broken window. His feet rested on the sill.

"Shakespeare!" I called, desperately. And then I tried to wheedle, "Come here, sweet boy. I have treats!"

He gave me a strange stare and then started through. Soon only his behind protruded from the broken window. Even worse, it was only big enough to fit him.

"Now what's he done?" Aunt Mattie wanted to know. With one hand, she leaned against the brick wall. I could see the exhaustion dragging her down. I had to get her somewhere to rest.

I'd never done a breaking and entering before. I hesitated.

"You can't leave the creature there alone, my girl. You'll have to go after him." Her voice was even tired.

"I can't get in."

"You aren't going to get into trouble; it's an abandoned building. Let's find something and bash in the glass of the door. We'll figure out how to get in from there."

"Yes, yes. You're right." I hated leaving the window and Shakespeare, but if I got the door open, I could grab him quickly. I walked around the dumpster and spotted a chunk of concrete jammed beneath a drain pipe. The chunk was heavy, but I managed to load it onto my shoulder and approached the door. With both hands, I lifted it overhead.

I groaned with the effort.

"My goodness! Are you okay?" she asked, scuttling over.

I didn't show that I heard her. Unreasonable or not, I was starting to feel like this was all her fault. "What was I thinking? Why do I let you drag me into this stuff?"

"Because you love me and want me to stay out of trouble?" she suggested.

"This is the last time."

"You said that the last time."

I waddled over with the chunk when she yelled, "Careful, dear! Stand back and throw it at the glass. The mesh in the glass will keep it from flying back too far."

For once, I did as I was told, and soon found the chunk had worked. The glass was shattered, but the mesh had held it together.

"Now you can whack at it," she offered.

Shakespeare meowed, fueling my urgency. I whacked furiously until the entire glass seemed to fold in upon itself.

Dank, cool air wafted out the opening.

"Shakespeare!" I shouted and waited. Nothing. I called again. Still no answer. "I swear, you'll spend the next month sleeping on the couch with the bedroom door shut when I get you." It was the worst punishment I could think of.

That brought him into the swath of light streaming inside, but still well out of reach.

"You'll have to get something to stand on and go in. Look in the dumpsters."

Dumpsters are repulsive things. They heave with odors, human and otherwise. I stared inside and hoped there was something inside I could stand on to get out. I was certifiable.

It took lifting the lids on four before I spotted some pallets stacked behind one. Thanking my stars I didn't need to climb inside, I dragged the pallets, one by one, and stacked them again against the door.

"How are you going to get back out?" Aunt Mattie called as I was about to lob myself, posterior over teakettle, as they say.

"I'll figure it out. If I don't come out, get help."

"But, it's time for lunch."

I poked my head out the window after making an awkward swan dive-ish entry into the warehouse. "If you leave me here, I'll tell on you," I threatened, a dark look on my face.

"Who would believe you?" she mocked.

She was right. No one would believe me. Certainly no one who happened to be passing by or was already in the building. I shivered at the thought and went in search of Shakespeare.

What I found was even worse than I'd imagined.

Chapter Three

From somewhere deep in my throat came a sound I'd never heard myself do before. A cross between a scream and a burp erupted out as I staggered back from the body on the floor. I'd seen my share of bodies, but nothing prepared me for the sight.

But worst of all was the coffee cup sitting next to him. That's what I remembered the most—he looked like someone you'd see sitting in a café.

My stomach lurched. I ran for the broken window of the door.

Aunt Mattie came toward the building and tapped on the door. "Are you all right? What happened? Open this up, immediately," she ordered.

"I'm okay!" I shouted, and then shook my head. Immediately, I turned my head and lost what was left of my stomach.

"Now open the door. And I have your cat!"

I stumbled over to the door and tried to operate it. "It's jammed."

There were two sharp raps, and then the door swung open, Aunt Mattie's hand still on the knob. "We might have tried this first before breaking that window. Now, show me what you found."

All I could do was point over in the general direction. I couldn't go back to the corpse.

She walked over with her usual matter-of-fact attitude. A very sweet Shakespeare curled around my ankles, trying to soothe me as if to say, "I'm sorry I got you into this." I scooped him up and buried my face in his fur.

She soon reappeared, holding out a lace-edged handkerchief. "My goodness. We will need to report this."

I nodded, but before I could take a step, she added, "But first, I want to look around."

"Whatever for?" I blurted, flabbergasted.

She gave me one of her signature looks, the one with a painted eyebrow raised. "You think they're just going to take our word for it that we happened to chase a cat in here and this is what we found?"

"But it's the truth," I said, exasperated.

"No one believes the truth, my girl. You know that."

She tottered away, and there was no choice but to follow her.

As I approached on the second attempt, handkerchief over my nose, I noticed the wall beyond the body. It was covered with graffiti, and at the base, in the dirt on the floor was the phrase, "Dead Words." It looked fresh.

"Oh!" I pulled back.

There was a flash as Aunt Mattie pulled out her ever-present camera. There were times I wished she wasn't as inquisitive as she was, but it was only because it brought us into such predicaments. Writing blogs for the Whiskers Cat Food Company was very vanilla compared to my adventures with her.

"What do you think that means?" I asked, nodding toward the wall.

She snapped another picture. "We will find out." She tip-toed around the area, being careful to stay back from the body. She must have taken twenty photos before she turned to me and said, "Before we go, Emily, do you have note paper on you?"

"Yes, I always carry it. Do you need it?"

"I'm afraid I'm feeling quite fatigued. I would love to stay longer, but age has defeated me. Take these notes for me, please?"

"Of course." I pulled out the paper, dug around in the bottom of my bag for a pen, and used my purse as a hard surface upon which to write. "Go ahead."

"The body was found lying on the floor. Arms and legs were sprawled apart, which leads me to believe that he may have been killed elsewhere and the body deposited here."

"Is that... it?" I felt my stomach rising again.

"No, there's more. Hold on, my girl. We're almost there." Aunt Mattie turned back to face the body and began speaking again. "I estimate the victim to be in his late twenties. Although his clothes are rumpled, they are of good quality. A coffee cup sits next to him that says Dutch Cup. His hair is well-trimmed, as are his nails. He is wearing Gucci shoes, quite expensive. Words have been written on the floor just beyond the body. They appear to be handwritten, and his hand is dirty. I see no other debris or clues lying around the body, although one cannot rule out forensic evidence that is not clearly visible to the eye. Judging from this distance, I would say the poor man died roughly a couple hours ago. It is now ten a.m. My niece, Emily, and I are leaving now to make a police report." She reached for my notes and added, signed, Mattie Lickenson. Her gaze flicked toward me. "Okay, that should do it. Let's leave."

"Finally." I couldn't get out of there soon enough. We walked past the empty lot and found a bench. Although we had walked to Shoetown, I insisted that we find a cab to take us to the police station. I could tell Aunt Mattie was at her end when it came to energy, although she'd never admit it.

Next to the lot, there was a young boy sitting on the front porch of his house. His curious gaze stared at us for a few moments. "What are you ladies doing out here?"

"Waiting for a cab," Aunt Mattie answered.

He broke into a grin, showing a missing top tooth. "Why don't you come up here on the porch and have a seat. My mom made some iced tea before she left for the grocery. I'll get you each a glass."

"Oh, you're so kind," Aunt Mattie called to him as she walked directly up the walkway and then settled into a white wooden rocker on his porch. "Oh, that feels so much better. I'm afraid I may have overdone it this time."

"You think?" I couldn't help being sarcastic. It had hardly been the relaxing walk she had promised.

The boy emerged from the house, handed each of us a glass of tea, and said,

Aunt Mattie took a deep drink and then smiled at the boy. "What's your name, young man?"

"Billy Thompson."

"How do you do, Billy? I'm Mattie Lickenson, and this is my niece, Emily. I wonder, Billy. Do you see a lot of activity going on in these old buildings nearby?"

His nose wrinkled, scrunching his freckles. "Maybe."

"How about this morning?"

He looked at the buildings and then back at Aunt Mattie. "Yes, but not anything I want to talk about."

She waved her hand. "Oh, I don't need specifics. I just wondered whether people come and go from here?"

"Yeah. I suppose so. My mom says not to talk to strangers." He eyed us suspiciously then.

"Quite wise, young man. Wise, indeed. It's just that..."

"Yes?" He couldn't help himself. Aunt Mattie was very good at this sort of thing.

"It's just thoughts. Well, I'm afraid we found something quite disturbing. I wouldn't want you to get in any trouble, of course, but I'm thinking that if you could remember seeing any particular cars or people coming in and out of that parking lot within the last day, that would be all the police would need to know. I'd make sure they leave you alone and no one would find out."

"Police? No lady, I don't want anything to do with the police." He started to back away from her, with his hand on the screen door. A second later, that door was shut, and I heard the lock click.

"Well, you've done it now," I mumbled.

"Yes, I have, haven't I? And it worked quite neatly." She stood up with a sigh and daintily set the glass on the rail of the porch. With a purposeful glance forward, she slowly descended the steps. "Come along, Emily," she called over her shoulder. "I believe our ride is headed this way."

Sure enough, a yellow cab pulled up to the curb. Aunt Mattie got inside. She waved at me to follow her.

I climbed in beside her. The cab driver gave Shakespeare a hard look but didn't say anything. Before I had my seatbelt buckled, I heard her order the cabby to take us to the police station.

Once we were underway, I couldn't restrain myself any longer. "Why did you do that?"

"What's that, my girl?"

"Why did you tell that kid we were going to the police? Naturally, he wouldn't talk to us after that."

"No, he won't talk to us, but he will talk to someone who will know who did the crime. I've planted the bait, and the killers will come looking for us." Her voice was quite matter of fact.

"What? Wait... what? You want the killers to come looking for us?"

"What easier way to uncover them?"

I swear, my life practically flashed before my eyes at the thought. I turned sideways on the seat and snapped my fingers so that she looked at me. "Hello? Aunt Mattie? That's completely bananas! You and I have no defense. We have no protection. Heck, the police in town don't even like us. They see you as a busybody who interferes where she shouldn't. I don't even know why we're going over there, except the law requires that we report it. We could've done that on the phone, you know? But no, not you. Not my aunt. You insist on telling them to their faces. You want to see their reaction, hear their discussion, put in your two cents' worth. And now? Now you want to lure the killers to us?" The last words came out in a squeak.

"Driver, step on it." She turned back toward me. "All these years and you still don't trust me. Don't you think I know what I'm doing?"

"No. I don't think you know what you're doing."

"Well, I do!" she snapped back and turned away, studiously staring out the window. "Driver, go on and don't stop again until we reach the precinct."

We had each retreated to our own thoughts. My mind was filled with things I wished to express, but out of respect for her age and our familial bond, I chose to keep them to myself.

Chapter Four

The driver had watched our fight in the rearview mirror. He decided to mention as he pulled over to the curb in front of the police station. "You sure this is where you want to go? Is it safe to let you two out? They might keep two squabblers like you."

"Very funny, young man," snapped Aunt Mattie. She sounded tough, but I could hear the tension in her voice. Instantly, I felt bad. I knew she was tired and still recovering from a recent leg break. I reached over and patted her arm. She didn't look at me directly, but she patted my hand in return, and I knew we were okay.

The precinct hadn't changed much since the last time we'd been there. It was a large building, by our local standards, and filled with prisoners sitting on old plastic benches. The hardened criminals were moved in and out of a rear entrance. It struck me as strange that one could be ushered in the front door, perfectly innocent, and disappear out the back, never to be heard from again. I have to admit, it made me hesitate on the door threshold.

Aunt Mattie was a familiar figure in the precinct, but not one who was welcomed with bouquets of flowers. No, my aunt was greeted by a rolling wave of raised eyebrows and sudden desires to hit the bathroom. I swear I even heard a groan from the back of the room.

Just as I'd expected, the room suddenly emptied, save for one younger officer I didn't recognize. "Yes, ma'am?"

"I'm Mattie Lickenson. Perhaps you've heard of me?"

He must have drawn the short straw. By the look on his face, though, it was obvious he'd heard of her. The expression was like he found a spider in his cornflakes.

Before he could respond, she spouted, "I have been here many times. I've solved many crimes. Surely you have heard of me." Her self-introduction was that of a celebrity expecting to be recognized.

"Uh, yes, yes. I've heard of you."

Oh, yes. Definitely the spider.

"Well, good. That's settled. You must know then that I've come to report a crime."

"Okay. What sort of crime?"

"A murder. You might be hesitant to give it that title, but by the looks of the victim and the scene, I hardly think he could have done himself in."

His eyebrows shot up. "A murder? Who? Where?" He swallowed hard, his Adam's apple sharply moving. "Let me get someone with more seniority."

"No."

"No?"

"Absolutely not." My aunt was unshakeable. "I'm quite done dealing with law enforcement who see me come in and run for the corners. I know them, young man. I know them all. I want to deal only with you. I won't tell anyone else, not a peep. And I won't even tell you unless I get your promise you'll work with me."

"Ma'am, I'm not sure I can do that."

"What did you say your name was?"

He pointed to the tag on his shirt.

"I can't see that from here, young man. What do you expect from eyes my age?"

He didn't answer, clearly flabbergasted. The police department learned to deal with all sorts of people, and I had a feeling this would be his lesson with someone like my aunt.

She squinted, still trying to read before finally giving up. "Well, anyway, you strike me as someone who needs to make some brownie points. Heaven knows everyone needs a bit of help climbing up the police force ladder. I'm just the one who can do that for you." She beamed at him like the Grandma from a pancake commercial.

He slowly shook his head, the hesitancy evident on his face. "Ma'am, I know you want to be a part of things. We all know about you here. I recognize why you'd like to work with me, because quite frankly, I have nothing to lose and plenty of time. And you're right, it won't hurt my resume to solve a murder. But, you're obligated by law to report murder to whoever here asks, be it me or my superior. I can't bargain with that. So, unless you tell me where the body is, I'm going to get the captain and will lock you up. So, what's it going to be?"

My inner voice was gasping. Aunt Mattie wasn't used to being talked to that way. She thought she was being very clever in her presentation. But she had been outsmarted by a young buck.

She raised her chin and gave him a steely glare. Dare I say, he gave it back.

After a moment, she smiled. "Young man, I respect your diligence. Yes, I will be happy to tell whoever I need to. And I know you will give me any information you legally can so that I can help you solve the crime."

His eyebrows raised. "Ma'am, if you don't mind my asking, why is it you want to be involved?"

"It's a matter of safety. My niece and I are already involved just by finding the body."

He nodded solemnly. "I understand." He tapped his chest. "And the name is Officer Timothy."

"Very well, then let's get on with it, shall we?"

Officer Timothy nodded and pulled a clipboard from beneath the counter. We watched as he walked to an opening in the counter, pushed open the swinging half-door, and nodded for us to follow. "No cats."

"But..."

"No cats."

I looked up at Officer Timothy. He was very tall, lean, and had a more than pleasant face. "I understand," I said. "You must, by all means, go by the rules. It's just that he's a well-behaved cat, a material witness in all this, and there's no one to watch him. I'll stay behind out here and wait while you deal with my aunt."

A little light came into his brown eyes. He rubbed beneath his nose in acknowledgment of my clever manipulation. "A witness, you say? Okay then. All witnesses follow me," he said and quickly walked toward the captain's office with Aunt Mattie, Shakespeare, and I in tow.

"Well, Emily," Aunt Mattie whispered. "It looks like we have a real mystery on our hands. I just know that Officer Timothy here will help us solve it in no time." She was trying to curry favor.

Officer Timothy spoke up. "Ma'am, I'm sure the captain will do his best to investigate the crime, but I'm here to make sure the investigation is conducted properly."

Aunt Mattie looked somewhat satisfied. "Oh, I'm sure the captain knows what he's doing. He just needs a little push in the right direction. Now, let's go in there and tell him what we know."

I was more concerned, but kept my mouth shut. At this point, I didn't want to dig us in any deeper.

Captain Wilson came in then. I noted his resigned expression in his down-turned mouth.

"What are you two doing here? And a cat? This is a precinct, not a tea party." His greeting was expected.

Aunt Mattie straightened her shoulders. "We are here to report a crime, Captain. We have come across a body in a warehouse in Shoetown. We think it's a murder." I was happy she didn't mention how he was one of those who'd disappeared from the bullpen when we entered.

Captain Wilson's doubt was obvious. "And where is this body?" He glanced at Timothy. "You taking the report?"

The young officer nodded. "Yes, sir."

"Very well. Go ahead and take down the facts and send a car over."

Officer Timothy nodded.

"And you," finished the Captain, pointing at Aunt Mattie, "can go home after you make your report. We'll take it from here."

I nodded. "Trust me, we will."

Captain Wilson patted Officer Timothy's shoulder in almost a fatherly way, as one would comfort a son sent to do a very unpleasant task.

Chapter Five

The report went quickly. Aunt Mattie offered the written testimony that we had jotted down, but the officer preferred to hear it from our mouths. Disgruntled, my aunt gave it to me and I shoved it in my pant's pocket, not an easy feat while juggling a cat.

All in all, it was relatively painless, and Officer Timothy soon sent us on our way. In fact, he went so far as to order the cab for us and watch us get inside.

I have to admit, he gave me quite a cute smile when he shut the door. And that distracted me from what Aunt Mattie had told the cab driver.

I should have known something was up, and in no time at all, I found myself once again staring at the entrance to the

Shoetown industrial area. "We're not supposed to be here. I thought we agreed to let the police handle this?"

"Those buffoons? Surely, you must be joking. You know they don't have a clue how to properly investigate a scene."

"And we have no permission to be there. Trespassing on a crime scene is against the law, you know."

"I distinctly heard doubt in the captain's voice that there had been a real crime. I was doing my duty, but it will be some time before they send anyone over. I just thought we'd have another look around before they get here."

"Oh, my goodness! How many laws do you intend to break today—and it's not even dinner time yet. You stay put in this cab. Driver, take us to the Mulberry Apartments, due west of here."

He tipped the rim of his cap. "Yeah, I know the place." He pulled away from the curb, but Aunt Mattie had already opened the door and was about to step out. I grabbed at her sleeve and shouted at the driver to stop.

"Get back in here! I swear, I'll take you straight over to the courthouse and have you declared incompetent," I threatened.

Aunt Mattie heaved a sigh. "You can't do that, my girl. I won't let you."

"You can't stop me. Why, half the police department would probably testify against you at this point."

She gave me a low-browed, half-smile. "You have been an accomplice to everything I've done the past few years. You can't condemn me without condemning yourself, my girl."

"You wouldn't...."

"If it comes to my freedom, you bet your last slice of pizza I'm going for it."

I knew how she had a secret love for pizza, so I knew she meant it. Desperately, I tried another tack. "Look, they will be here at any minute. That alley has only one way in, and the scene of the crime will trap you inside. You'll foul the evidence, and they will catch us for sure." I noticed that I'd used the pronoun "we" when I meant to say "you." I was worried about my own mindset.

"We'll have the cab drive us right up to the entrance, and we won't stay longer than five minutes – I promise."

"No, I refuse." I crossed my arms over my chest.

"The longer you argue, the closer they're coming. I'm going in, with or without you." Aunt Mattie was the most confoundedly determined woman you could ever hope not to meet. But she had a point. Then she softened a bit. "I promise I'll be quick. There's just one more thing I want to see."

"Okay, fine! Driver, turn down that entrance until we signal you. And hurry."

He looked up in the rearview mirror and pulled his cap down low over his eyes, an excited grin on his face. "Oh, goody. I always wanted to drive the getaway car."

I rolled my eyes, and within seconds we were outside the door where I'd broken the glass. I jumped out and began wiping at the handle and edges of the window with the sleeve of my sweater. Aunt Mattie calmly toddled up behind me. "It won't do any good, my girl. They already know you were here. They'll accuse you of tampering with evidence."

I stopped mid-swipe. Hadn't I just used that same logic on her? I was losing my mind.

She reached around me and pushed the door open, sailing inside as though she were taking a walk around the block.

This time I already knew what to expect, and I might be uncovering clues that could save my own hide, so I paid extra attention. "Dead Words" stood out as though written in neon. Aunt Mattie was taking more pictures.

"Look!" I said, pointing. I'd spotted a wallet. Aunt Mattie wasted no time whipping out her lace-edged hankie and picking it up. My mouth froze open. She knew she wasn't supposed to be doing that, but nothing I could say would dissuade her. I kept quiet just to get her out as soon as possible. Aunt Mattie quickly went through the wallet, pulling out the bills and a few slips of paper.

"Hurry!" I urged her. In the distance, I heard the moan of a siren, and it was coming closer. She heard it too and quickly re-assembled the wallet and placed it back where she found it. Aunt Mattie was determined, but not stupid.

She turned, nodded to the door, and quickly herded me out of the warehouse and into the cab.

The driver looked down the alley. "Too late," he said, spotting the flashing lights of the cruiser advancing on us.

"Get down!" he barked, and we automatically slid flat upon the seat. He pulled up behind a dumpster and we waited as our lives passed before our eyes.

Chapter Six

"I mean it! Don't let them see you. Get down!" the cab driver yelled again. He needn't have said it. We were as flat as pancakes in the back seat, with me trying to keep Shakespeares tail out of my mouth.

There, in the cramped, shadowy space of the cab, time seemed to stretch forever as we waited. But luck, it appeared, was on our side. The police car, with its flashing lights and blaring sirens, was so focused on reaching the crime scene that they failed to notice our hideout. The officers drove by without slowing down, their attention solely on the warehouse entrance.

Our driver stayed silent, his eyes fixed on the rearview mirror until the cruiser was well past us. Only then did he let out a breath. He slowly eased the cab from behind the dumpster, the tires crunching softly on the gravel as we made our escape. With careful movements, he guided the cab down the road, ensuring not to draw any unnecessary attention.

Aunt Mattie, who had been craning her neck to watch the drama unfold through the back window, finally turned around. Her double chin quivered slightly with the motion, and she muttered with a wry smile, "Sometimes, I appreciate their incompetence." Her voice carried a mix of relief and amusement, a testament to her seasoned experience in such escapades.

I could not have agreed more. The relief of not being caught was overwhelming. We were safe, for now, heading back toward the comfort of home, our adventure at Shoetown momentarily behind us.

I didn't speak any more until we got back to my apartment before discussing the case any further. The cab driver was unknown to me, so it seemed to be the best idea to keep my cards close to my chest.

Once home, I fell onto the sofa. Shakespeare ran away to go hide on my bed. He needed some alone time after this morning's adventure, landing on my chest begging me for attention. "Whew, that was a close call. I can't believe we almost got caught by the police."

Aunt Mattie looked equally exhausted, if not more so. "I know, it's a good thing that cab driver was able to lose them. I don't think we would have been able to talk our way out of that one. I made sure he got a nice tip for his trouble."

"Speaking of trouble, we need to be careful from now on. We can't let our curiosity get the best of us like that again."

For once, Aunt Mattie looked properly chastised. "I know, you're right. I just couldn't resist the opportunity to take a closer look at that vacant building. I had a feeling we missed something."

"Well, it looks like your hunch paid off. We found that wallet and those other clues, but we have to be more cautious in the future." I felt bad, like I was kicking a dead horse. I knew she felt bad about exposing me to so much trouble.

"I know, I promise I'll be more careful."

I stared at her, feeling suspicious. She looked at me, as innocent as could be. "You sure about that?"

"Of course! You're right. Thanks for always looking out for me, Emily."

I didn't know if I believed her, but maybe it was true. "That's what family is for. Now, are you hungry? I can whip up some lunch." I stood up and went to the kitchen.

"That would be lovely. Tuna salad, maybe? Besides, we didn't come away empty-handed, at least. We saw the wallet." Her attempt at reform hadn't lasted too long.

I reached for the can of tuna. "Did you have time to look at it?"

"No, not really," she said, her voice dropping.

I turned to stare at her. "You did, didn't you?"

"Emily! I would never do anything illegal."

I groaned and rattled through the utensil drawer for the can opener. "What have you done, Aunt Mattie?" At the sound of the opener, Shakespeare came running.

She patted her purse with a kind of assuredness only she could muster, her gaze piercing through her jeweled glasses like a cat eyeing a particularly interesting mouse. "Just took pictures, like you saw."

"Are you going to show me?" I asked, my curiosity piqued, but also dreading the inevitable shenanigans.

Now she clutched her purse even closer to her side, as if it contained the crown jewels rather than just a phone with some incriminating photos. "You don't need to be an accessory. Now call me another cab."

"Why didn't you take that one home with you?" I couldn't

help but quip, knowing full well the answer would involve some cloak-and-dagger reasoning.

She gave me a look that could wither plants, her voice dripping with mock indignation. "I certainly didn't want him knowing where I lived. Can you imagine? Next thing you know, he'd be selling tickets to tour 'The House of Mattie Lickenson: Crime Scene Investigator Extraordinaire.'"

I chuckled, picturing the cab driver setting up a little tour stand outside her quaint, unsuspecting home. "Oh, that would be quite the entrepreneurial venture. 'Step right up, folks, see where the master sleuth plies her trade!'"

She joined in with a laugh, her stern demeanor cracking like the thin veneer of legality she often danced upon. "Exactly, and I'd have to start charging for autographs. No, thank you. The fewer people who know my home address, the better. Now, about that sandwich...?"

I shook my head as I reached for the bread. "Alright, alright. But don't think this gets you off the hook for the wallet caper."

After lunch, we called a new cab, and soon she was off. I looked at my computer, standing pitifully unused. Aunt Mattie would be on her own from that point forward. I had work to do.

Chapter Seven

Another morning, another phone call.

"Are you awake, girlie?" Aunt Mattie said. This time, she was mocking me since it was nearly noon.

"Yes, of course."

"Just pulling your leg, my dear. I need to come over. I have some news."

I stared at my computer in panic. "I have some writing to do. I'm behind." Then hope sparked me. "Are you going to show me the pictures?"

She ignored my question. "Oh, pooh. You know what I say about that. I have plenty of money to—"

"And you know I love to write."

"Well, how about in a couple of hours?"

I didn't think that would be enough time, but I was happy to end the argument. "Fine. I'll see you then."

"I'll see you with bells on!"

I managed to knock off a half-dozen blog posts and sent them in. I was all set for the week. It felt like stocking up on groceries and was especially satisfying.

In fact, I even had time to throw in a batch of oatmeal cookies and had them waiting, along with her favorite tea, when she rang my apartment. I buzzed her in. Her step on the stairwell rang throughout the building. She finally rounded the landing and stomped to my apartment door. I opened it immediately.

"What news do you have?" she asked.

I wanted to reply with, "My news? What's yours?" But that could make her clam up. So, instead I tried with a bit of sugar, "Come on in, Aunt Mattie. I've baked cookies and have your favorite tea."

That seemed to mollify her. She headed inside and headed for her favorite chair. Shakespeare was sitting in it and gave a grumpy look, but scooted over for her. "So, where are the refreshments?" she demanded, barely seated.

"Right here." I came from behind her with a tray and settled it on the ottoman before her. I handed her a cup of tea and a plate with two cookies on it. She added two more and then settled back, using her bosom as a temporary table. With a nibble, she sampled the cookie and gave a little moan of appreciation. "I don't know how you plan to keep a man if you ever get one, but those cookies will make a good start."

"Thank you," I answered in a cheery voice, refusing to take the bait. At that moment, my cell phone buzzed. "Hold on, Auntie."

"Hello?" I answered.

"Is this Emily Lickenson?"

The voice was male but unfamiliar. "Uh, yes."

"This is Brandon Timothy... Officer Timothy from the precinct?" He voiced it as a question, almost as if he wasn't quite sure who he was.

"Yes, Officer. How may I help you?"

"Oh, this isn't an official call," he hurried on to say.

"No? I'm sorry, I don't follow." I looked toward Aunt Mattie with upraised eyebrows, and her response was intense scrutiny. Quickly, I turned my back toward her.

"Well, I know this is rather unexpected, but I happen to have ended up with two tickets to dinner theatre at the Golden Palace, that popular place downtown?"

Again, the question. "Yes, I'm familiar with it."

"I was hoping you might like to accompany me."

I choked on my tongue. I hadn't been prepared. "Uh..."

"Oh, I know it's short notice. Saturday night. About seven?"

"Well..."

Aunt Mattie was, if anything, born to be my cheerleader. As I looked in her direction, she was making greatly exaggerated nods of her head, her arms sweeping in circles to indicate I should go along with things. How did she know? For all she knew, he could be asking me for a recipe for drain cleaner.

There was a knee-knocking silence on the other end. I hadn't thought about Officer Timothy since the day at the precinct. Oh, who was I kidding? I hadn't thought about anyone else. Even Aunt Mattie was not privy to my personal internal thoughts. One look at her smirk told me she was pretty good at guessing, though.

"Actually, I would like that," I said finally, giving in with as much grace as I could muster, given that Aunt Mattie was waving like a cheerleader across the room. For a moment, she'd forgotten her ailments. She was as flexible as a twenty-year-old when she wanted to be. "Shall I meet you there?"

"Oh, no. I would come and take you. I'll be at your apartment at 6:45, if that's okay?"

"Yes, very okay. See you then."

I set down the phone, stars flitting about in my chest. I caught a glimpse of myself in the mirror and could see that I was quite flushed.

"Well? Did he say they'd found the killer?"

"Oh, stop, will you? You know perfectly well he asked me on a date."

"The question is, do you know it's a date? After all, it's been a while since you left your apartment for a night out. Your cat will miss you!"

I thought about that. Shakespeare hated being alone and had a way of getting even. "Speaking of Shakespeare. Would you mind if he stays the night with you?"

Her mouth formed a round circle. I knew she would misunderstand what I was saying, and I had done it deliberately. It was my turn to shock her once in a while.

"No, I can't do that, I'm afraid. You know my dog hates felines."

The dog loved Shakespeare. "Well, then, perhaps I should ask Mrs. Pittmore to take him. Actually, I think I would like that better. I wouldn't have to hear all the complaining, and she may be very interested in how my date went." Yes, I knew I was being cruel, but with Aunt Mattie, sometimes you just had to be.

"All right, very well. I'll take the cat. It may get me kicked out of my apartment, though, so be prepared when I show up at your door with my suitcase in hand."

"If you do, I shall merely take you back and introduce you to your new roommate, Mrs. Pittmore."

"Stop with this. Now then. I came for a purpose, and let's get about it. Sit down here so that I may show you what I found."

In my shock over the phone call, I'd forgotten about the pictures. Still, I congratulated myself in my sugar technique. She pulled a stack of papers from her abnormally large handbag. Handing them over to me, she sat back to await my response.

"What are these?"

"Those? Well, those are printouts from the pictures I took. From the wallet that was 'spilled open.'" She did air quotes around the last two words. "As you can see, I did a very thorough job, especially with you breathing down my neck. I got a clear shot of almost everything in that wallet."

"Aunt Mattie, if the police knew you had these, you'd be spending the night in jail."

"But they're not going to find out about that, are they, dear niece?"

She had me, there. I was in checkmate. She knew that if I told Officer Timothy what she had done, he would be forced to call it a conflict of interest and my date would be off. I had no choice but to cooperate.

"That's just a little ironic, don't you think, coming from you?"

The smile she returned could have threatened a Cheshire cat. She motioned to the sheaf of copies. "Go on. Look at them."

Feeling the cold of the metal jail door slowly closing on me felt almost real as I looked at the documents I had no business seeing. "So, what am I looking at?"

"Well, the first thing that should jump right out at you is his business card."

I leafed through it until I saw what seemed to be a business card, although it was enlarged. My mouth dropped open as I read it. "Oh, my gosh, he's a professional blogger."

Aunt Mattie's heavy face bobbed up and down in a nod. "You see? It was worth the danger. Do you realize how much that narrows down our search?"

"But Aunt, we can't let on that we know this. They'll catch us for sure."

"No, dear, that's the whole point. His profession was the same as what you play around doing. As far as I'm concerned, you heard about his death through business circles."

"I can't believe the depths to which you will sink."

"Well, someone sunk even deeper, or we wouldn't be here having this conversation."

I nodded, my eyes half-closed. She made a point. I knew our safety depended on our thoroughness, but somehow I felt slightly better about that now that I knew Officer Timothy was interested in my welfare. That's when I realized I'd better keep Aunt Mattie at a distance when I was around him. She had the definite ability to muck things all up. She grabbed the papers from me.

"You are wasting my time, my girl."

"No, Aunt, I'm just thinking. Let me see those again." She shoved them at me, and I went back to the enlargement of his business card. "David Porter. That was his name, David Porter."

"Well, I'm glad to see you noticed something in all of that. Yes, Porter. Why?"

"Oh, nothing." I rubbed the back of my neck with one hand. It was a gesture I caught myself doing often when I had intense thinking to do. "It's just that it sounds so familiar."

"Familiar?" Her mouth dropped. "How? Do you know him?"

"I'm not sure. There's something about the name. Hold on." I ran to my desk and flipped on the computer. The deep dong it always made had such a sound of authority. I clicked on a few icons and then read. I drew in my breath.

"What? What have you found?"

"I knew the name was familiar. David Porter was a blogger who worked freelance, just like me. In fact, we both belonged to a social media group. Oh my gosh," I whispered.

"What? What?"

"If I'm not mistaken, he also contributed to the Whisker Treats company." I drew back, my hand going to the back of my neck again, lifting my hair and letting it slide as a wave off the back of my hand.

"Do you mean to tell me, you worked with him?"

I shook my head. "Not in the strictest sense. But, we did the same thing."

"Then you can track him down? Find out where he lived?"

I looked at her, my head spinning. "I definitely will try."

CEECEE JAMES

Aunt Mattie sat forward in her chair. "We might survive this yet. Call them. Now. Don't waste any time."

I glanced at the clock. "No, I think this is something I need to do in person, and it's too late today. Tomorrow is Saturday, so it will have to wait until Monday."

"When are you going on your date?"

"I already told you. Tomorrow night. You're taking my cat, remember?"

"Don't let on to the cop, my girl. You have to keep this all locked up tight." She mimed locking up her lips and throwing away the key.

"Oh, I know. Don't worry. I won't breathe a word."

"What if he asks you directly?"

"I don't know. I won't lie—I never lie, you know. But, there are creative ways of not answering. I learned them from you, as a matter of fact."

"Well, I'm glad you were listening at least some of the time," she snapped. "How about the rest of the evidence?"

"What's in this picture?" I couldn't make it out.

"Those are prints that led away from the body. It escaped me the first time, but the light had changed when we got back."

"Footprints? Are you sure? They're far too small to be prints."

"I never said they were human."

Her eyes were glittering, and I knew what that meant. She had happened onto another part of the puzzle but wasn't ready to share her suspicions. Not yet. I nodded and let it go. "No, I don't see much. Let's wait to see what I can learn on Monday. For now, let me bag up the rest of those cookies, and I'll have Shakespeare over to you at noon. I'll bring his food and his bed, of course."

She opened her mouth to protest, but I dished out one of her own signature Aunt Mattie looks, and she snapped it shut. Even she couldn't argue with the prospect of breaking the case, and at that point, I had the best shot of uncovering a very important clue.

I swung around toward Shakespeare. "You hear that? You get to go spend the night at Aunt Mattie's," I cooed.

"You better get along with Al Cabone," she said, naming her dog.

"You have my house key, right?"

"Of course," she quipped. "I am anything if not efficient."

I picked up the remote and soon found our favorite show. When it was over, I called her cab and packed her off with the rest of the cookies when it came.

Then it was time to tackle my wardrobe. It was an absolute disaster zone, looking like a tornado had hit a thrift store and left only the '90s fashion behind, clearly showcasing my work-from-home chic. I knew I had to make a break for the shops unless I wanted to show up to the theater in pajamas with coffee stains.

The theater! Oh, the thrill! It was so exciting, I could barely contain my excitement, which meant I spent the night tossing and turning, dreaming of popcorn and not the popcorn ceiling above my bed.

Chapter Eight

"Shakespeare!" I called in my sweetest voice.

He knew something was up. He always knew. I had tried to hide the cat kennel at the end of the counter, but he knew, and detested the sight of it.

I crinkled the treat bag in an enticing way and shook the bag. When there was no response, I took it to the living room, far away from the kennel, and shook it again. Waving his tail, he came out to stare at me. I offered him the bag.

Not even a brief sniff. Oh, dear. I was in trouble now. I scattered a few around the floor. Then, I dug out his favorite toys from under the sofa. Hopefully, that would appease him when Aunt Mattie came to pick him up.

"Be a good boy," I said, grabbing my purse. I left him nibbling one, and hope he'd be okay. I didn't worry about Aunt Mattie having trouble collecting him. Everyone obeyed my aunt, even my cat.

I couldn't describe how excited I was about the thought of heading to the theater. It was the most liberated I'd felt since I'd become an adult. It felt wonderful.

The feeling began to ebb as I drove. It had been so long since I bought myself a dress. I didn't even know what was in style anymore.

Nervously, I walked into the store. Just as I thought, I immediately felt overwhelmed by the vast collection of dresses. My gaze darted around, unsure of where to start until a bright, yellow dress caught my eye.

Just as I reached out to grab it, a friendly sales lady approached me, looking impeccably put together. I half wanted to ask her to find me what she was wearing.

"That's a beautiful dress," she said with a kind smile. "Where are you heading, and what kind of look are you going for?"

With a deep breath, and in a rush I explained to her about my dinner theatre date. My cheeks warmed as I confessed it was my first in years.

Her eyes lit up, and she giggled delightedly. "Oh, that sounds like fun! Let's find you something spectacular." She then led me through different racks, her enthusiasm infectious.

As we walked, she asked, "Do you want something bold or more classic?"

"I think I'd like something that's in style but with a bit of charm," I replied, trying to picture my evening.

"And who is this mysterious date?"

"A police officer."

"Oh," she said approvingly, then pulled out a dress with a gentle sweep of her hand. "This one has a vintage charm but with modern flair. Try this on."

It was a no-go, but she was determined to help me. After trying several options, we finally found it - a dress that was the perfect blend of elegance and whimsy. It was a soft blue, flowing gracefully with intricate detailing at the waist.

"This one," I said with a smile, feeling a surge of confidence.

"Oh, yes. I agree!" She smiled, pleased. "This one will make him forget all about his police radio," she added, making me laugh.

"Thanks to you, I might actually feel like I belong at the theatre tonight," I admitted, grateful for her help.

She beamed, "You're going to be the star of the show, dear."

When I got home, I saw that Aunt Mattie had proven to be faithful and packed Shakespeare to her home. She left a note, "This house has been cleaner." She proved this by drawing a smiley face in the dust on top of my microwave.

I rolled my eyes and crumpled the note. Then I laid out the dress on the bed. After admiring it for a moment, I tried it all on, including a pair of shoes I'd splurged on at the last minute.

I looked at myself in the full-length mirror. The reflection was not of the person who had walked into the store an hour earlier. The dress hugged my body in all the right places, accentuating my curves, while the shoes added sophistication to my silhouette.

A slight flush filled my cheeks at how different I looked—almost like I was wearing someone else's confidence. But that feeling was quickly overshadowed by a surge of pride and joy. I stood there, marveling at my transformation, feeling ready to embrace the night ahead with Officer Timothy.

***

The buzzer rang at precisely 6:45. I buzzed him in and quickly refreshed my lipstick while I waited. A minute later, there was a knock, and I opened the door to find Officer Timothy standing there, wearing civilian clothes and filling them out quite well.

"Hi," I said, feeling a little reserved. I straightened my spine and smiled.

"Hello," Brandon answered, looking me over. "You look lovely," he said, and I felt myself flush.

"I see you like to be prompt," I said awkwardly.

"Yes, it seems I'm always on time," he said with a smile. And then his expression straightened. "I want to get this out of the way. We've identified the victim you found. I don't want to get into it, but I do want to confirm it was murder. Toxic poisoning."

I nodded, unsure of where to go from here.

He smiled again. "I just thought I'd get that out in the open. But, from here on, it's just you, and me, okay?"

I nodded. Then he added a little cagey, "Of course, if you remember anything else about that morning, you can tell me. Tomorrow. Business hours."

That made me laugh. It was quickly cut off when he added, "Your Aunt Mattie mentioned that you were hesitant about tonight's event. Would you like to talk about it?"

"She did? When did you talk to her?"

"We talked earlier this morning, actually," Brandon said. "She was kindly concerned about how you were feeling."

I covered my mouth. "My aunt called you at the precinct? Oh, how embarrassing."

Brandon chuckled and said, "It's all right. I'm sure your aunt was just looking out for you. A good quality to have in this day and age."

"You don't know my aunt," I answered as he helped me on with my coat.

"Oh, you might be surprised. I have my share of aunts, too."

"Really? What are they like? What kind of things do they do?" I asked, intrigued.

"My guess is that most aunts are pretty much alike. Busy bodies and even busier mouths."

"Yes, I'd say that covers it." We grinned at each other.

The breeze felt cool on my skin as the sun began to set. We hopped in Brandon's compact car and drove off to the theater. The streets were buzzing with people this weekend night.

Brandon turned up the radio, and we talked about our favorite pop songs from our childhood as he weaved through traffic. Upon arriving at the theater, he checked his wallet to make sure we had the tickets.

We made our way to the ticket booth, and he handed the girl two tickets for the comedy show that was currently running.

Upon entering, I was instantly captivated by all of the colorful sets and costumes on stage—it looked like something straight out of a fairytale!

We found our seats at center stage for an optimal view of all of the actors. Brandon offered me some popcorn, but I wasn't hungry yet, so I kindly declined. I knew he'd keep it safe till later if I got peckish during the show itself. I guessed that his idea of dinner, and mine, were different. I straightened my dress and tried not to feel overdressed.

The house lights dimmed gradually until eventually it was pitch black, with only rainbows of colors pouring out from each projector onto a giant white wall in front of us.

And I did end up sharing his popcorn after all.

Chapter Nine

Popcorn or no popcorn, when we stepped out of the theater, my stomach embarrassed me by growling with hunger.

Brandon was a gentleman and didn't mention it. He did, however, drop a casual, "How about dinner?"

I eagerly agreed, probably too eagerly but I was starving.

We hopped back into his car, drove for a few minutes, and pulled up to a local restaurant that Brandon had heard about from some of his friends. It looked small but warm and inviting, and the smells emanating from inside were truly amazing.

Brandon came around and opened my door. Then he reached for my hand, and we walked into an atmosphere full of laughter and conversation. We were guided to a table near the corner window.

Our waiter arrived shortly after with menus and a welcoming smile, telling us all about the day's specials. "You've got to try the wings; they're famous here," he suggested.

We decided to get a mix of dishes so we could try as much as possible: fiery wings, creamy mashed potatoes, freshly baked pizza, and tangy coleslaw.

Brandon went ahead and ordered a beer for himself while I opted for a glass of raspberry lemonade.

"This is just what I needed after the theater," I said, taking a refreshing sip.

As we waited for our food to arrive, we got caught up in harmless banter about work projects and current events. I was very careful to steer away from anything close to Shoetown or dead bodies.

"Did you see that article about the new tech hub downtown?" Brandon asked, his eyes lighting up with interest.

"No, but I heard about it. Could be good for business," I replied, feeling the evening's pace slow into a comfortable rhythm.

Soon enough, our food arrived in giant portions, just waiting for us to dig in! We ate until neither one of us could manage another bite; somehow we'd managed to clear all the plates without even realizing how much time had passed by.

We chatted some more over dessert—sugary treats are always great conversation starters.

"This chocolate cake is incredible," I said, savoring each bite.

"And the tiramisu? Chef's kiss," Brandon added, making an exaggerated kissing gesture that made both of us laugh.

By now, it was getting quite late, but neither of us wanted our time together to end. Reluctantly, however, Brandon eventually checked his watch. "I should probably drive you home. I've got to work early tomorrow," he said, a hint of disappointment in his voice.

"Yeah, you're right," I sighed, not wanting the night to conclude but knowing it was necessary. I gathered my things, while he paid the bill, and then we stepped back into the cool night air.

Later, we said goodbye outside of my apartment building with farewell hugs lingering just slightly longer than normal before finally separating ways. My heart pounded, hoping he thought the date was as much of a success as I did.

I lay in bed with a smile plastered on my face and thoughts of Brandon constantly racing through my head.

On one hand, I almost wished that time would stand still so that I could savor every moment; on the other, I already couldn't wait to spend more time with him. After all, it seemed like we shared many common interests and had hit it off right away.

I turned onto my side and tried counting sheep to force myself to sleep, but even that got boring. All I could think about was Brandon! What's his favorite color? What kind of books does he read? Did he love animals?

My mind kept skittering from one topic to another as if eager for answers before eventually shifting its focus toward Shoetown. David Porter, fellow blogger.

Why would someone do that to you?

With a groan, I hit my pillow. Back to detective work again.

Chapter Ten

Sunday afternoon found me eagerly awaiting a call from Brandon. We hadn't talked since our wonderful date the night before. I tried to remind myself that he said he was at work, but honestly, it was driving me crazy.

Suddenly, my phone buzzed with an incoming call. I couldn't help the stab of apprehension to see that it was Aunt Mattie. She'd be grilling me about my date for sure.

"Good morning!" I greeted, trying to keep my voice neutral.

"Good morning, Emily. Awake already? Anyone stay over for breakfast?" she asked with her usual curiosity.

I bit back a groan. I'd already prepared myself for this, but her breakfast comment caught me off guard. "Oh, it was fine,"

I said, hoping a simple answer would satisfy her. "And how was Shakespeare and Al Capone?"

To my surprise, Aunt Mattie seemed content with that answer. Usually, she would keep asking questions, trying to pry into my private life. "They were fine. He was a lovely distraction during game night. I won, I'll have you know," she said, her voice brimming with pride.

"Wow, that's great! What game did you play?"

"Oh, it was a good old game of Scrabble. I had an amazing word with 'Quixotic'—landed me a triple word score," she recounted with a chuckle.

I laughed, genuinely happy for her. "You've always had a way with words."

"You know that's true. Anyway, I'm letting you know that I'll be popping over in a bit to bring you your cat."

"Can you manage the kennel?"

"Emily, I might be eighty, but like my father used to say, I'm built like a Clydesdale!"

I laughed. "Thanks for watching him, Aunt Mattie. He can be destructive if he gets left alone."

"I well remember," she said dryly, silently reminding me she had once fostered him. "He found my slippers again like they were his long lost cousins. Anyway, aside from those, he was a good boy and earned his keep. And you don't even have to give me last night's scoop," she said charitably and hung up. I laughed as I returned the phone to the table. Time would tell if she could keep that promise.

Brandon could call or not. I felt better about it.

So it was funny when the phone rang again, and it was him. Despite me talking myself down, my heart raced as soon as I heard his voice.

We exchanged pleasantries, and then he asked me how my day was going; I stammered a bit, partly because of my emotions and trying to play it cool.

We talked for a few minutes. Eventually, we said goodbye, both agreeing to talk again soon. As soon as I hung up, I couldn't help but notice that my cheeks hurt from so much smiling.

I'd just prepared the water for tea. I'd given my aunt all the left-over cookies, so, for a treat, I decided to make cinnamon toast. I knew she loved it as much as I did.

The toaster had just popped up when she buzzed. I rang her in, unlocked the door, and started to butter the treat. She let herself in with an appreciative sniff. "Smells lovely! Now, time to get back to work."

She set down my cat, who immediately ran to my room. He needed alone time again.

"I have one thing to tell you, Brandon confirmed that David was indeed murdered."

Aunt Mattie shook her head as she reached for the cinnamon. "Well, we knew that was true, the poor man. Now get that computer of yours open."

The two of us sat huddled over my laptop and typed in the phrase "Dead Words" just to see what would come up. I tried to ignore the little sugar grains scattering across the keyboard when she adjusted her glasses and leaned in close.

Unfortunately, "Dead Words" yielded nothing but dead ends.

I sighed, pushing back from the table. "We need another hint."

Aunt Mattie nodded, her eyes scanning the room as if searching for inspiration. "Let's look into the victim, David Porter. He was a blogger, right?"

We turned our attention to the victim's online presence, and soon found his private social media account. It turned out to be a treasure trove of information, detailing David's recent public clash with a fellow employee over the company's practices.

Aunt Mattie pointed to a blog post. "My goodness. He

certainly had a temper. Look at this heated argument with someone at your work. This could be key."

I nodded, my memory jogged. "I do remember something about that, only from the other person, Mitch. It was intense."

We kept digging into the argument. There was an anonymous person commenting, just named 'media user'. This person sent a few cryptic threats. David Porter wrote back with cutting remarks.

Aunt Mattie said, her voice low. "Do you think this has to do with that argument you heard about? Maybe 'Dead Words' is some kind of code or threat related to his posts."

I then did some quick typing and we found the social media accounts of David's family. It made me feel a bit icky looking at them, but I was hoping for some personal insight into his enemy.

"My brother believed he was onto something big just before he died," the sister wrote. "Maybe too big. I can't believe this happened again."

I turned to Aunt Mattie, my determination unwavering. "Happened again? That's weird."

"Weird is as weird does. First thing we have to find out what 'Dead Words' means. I swear this whole thing has my mind is racing, and that's not good at my age." She patted my hand. "You keep digging, girl. I know you can do it. Find the truth behind a blogger's murder. And there's one place you can hear it best. Right from the horse's mouth."

I nodded. My office was the next visit.

Chapter Eleven

I rarely had to make an appearance at the office, but every once in a while, there was no escaping it. I knew, after last night, my next task was to play detective with the office crew. I needed to see if anyone could recall David Porter, or his fight.

The cement building was one of those boring three-story ones you see in every city. Whisker Treats Cat Food Company rented the second floor. I took the stairs and walked inside.

Here, the room was filled with desks and quiet typing. I swear I could feel the creative energy in the air.

At the front desk sat the personnel director, Sheila. She was a plain woman with an unassuming presence that likely made her perfect for her job. My main memory of her was her snobby indifference when I'd interviewed for the job.

Sheila didn't look up when I approached.

"Hello," I said. "My name is..."

Apparently, nothing about her attitude had changed. Before I even finished introducing myself, she immediately cut me off with a wave of her hand. "What do you want?" Her voice had an edge to it, insinuating I was a bother.

I pushed forward with my mission. "I heard that David Porter worked for you as a blogger. Do you know anything about him?"

Sheila's eyes narrowed. Apparently, she didn't appreciate my question. Even more awkward, the glare continued without her responding. I waited through an uncomfortable beat of silence until I could see she wasn't going to answer. I thanked her before turning to leave.

Then I remembered Aunt Mattie. She'd never take a no for an answer, especially when it was important to David's family to find out what happened to him. They deserved the truth. Straightening my spine, I turned back.

"I know you're probably busy," I said, trying to make my voice sound firm. "But I really need to get some information about

David and his work history. It's extremely important." I showed her my work badge. I wasn't ready to let out that he had died.

Sheila actually rolled her eyes before finally sighing. "Fine," she said gruffly. "Go talk to her." She pointed to another lady, this one obviously an intern by the way she buzzed about from desk to desk.

The brunette gave me a quick smile as I walked up. "I know you! Emily Lickenson! I recognize your face from your blog profile picture."

"Oh, hi!" I said. "What's your name?"

"Martha." She blushed. "I just started work here."

"Glad to meet you. Sheila suggested I talk to you about another co-worker."

"Sheila," she snickered. "I'm surprised you got her to talk at all."

I laughed, and we had a camaraderie bond.

"What's the name?"

"David Porter."

"Oh." Her expression changed as her eyebrows lowered in sadness. "I heard. Absolutely terrible."

I nodded.

"Drug overdose. Such a horrible way to go," she continued. "Gary told us this morning."

"I'm sorry," I said, feeling bad. I wondered about calling his death an overdose. The police must be keeping it being murder under wraps.

"I didn't know him well, but every time I talked with him, he was always nice. I think we're all in shock." She took in a deep breath. "What do you need?"

"Any information to help figure out what happened."

She thought for a moment, tapping her chin. "Here, follow me. I know what can help."

Quickly, she led me through the desks, and I carefully followed her. I say careful because at one point I tripped over someone's crutch they had leaning next to the chair.

I quickly apologized to the man and received a "don't worry about it," but my cheeks flamed with embarrassment. We walked in silence the rest of the way (for which I was thankful) until we arrived at a big filing cabinet at the far corner of the room. She opened it up and gestured for me to take a look inside.

I realized I'd hit the mother lode. This was where all of

Whisker Treats' blogger employment records were kept. Mine were probably in that drawer as well.

"I hope you'll find what you're looking for here," she said, her voice soft. "It's terrible what happened to him." She gave me a warmish smile before returning to her errands.

I rapidly shuffled through David's file until I found an article he wrote. A paystub was paperclip to the top. Scribbled across the top of the article was the phrase "Dead Words." I scanned the article quickly as my heart pounded with excitement.

It turned out to be something to do with empty promises cat food manufacturers make. Frowning, I tried to understand what about it would be linked to the words. But there was nothing.

I glanced at the paystub and saw the amount was for a years worth of work. Discouraged, I replaced the both and headed out.

I waved in Sheila's direction as I left, but she didn't look up. Leaving Whisker Treats, I felt newfound determination, now armed with David's address. Surely, there was nothing standing between me and finding out what happened to him once and for all.

There was one stickler in the entire situation. I knew for certain that it was David's body we'd come across. No positive identification had been made, as far as I was aware. Brandon hadn't even given me the name.

Was his drug use well known?

Chapter Twelve

Shakespeare was glad to see me when I returned home, as he proved by nearly tripping me as I ran for the bathroom.

When I finished, I gave him another snack for being such a good boy. Then I brushed him. He seemed extra spunky when I finished, probably bored from me being gone all morning.

"Alright, buddy, you feel like a walk?"

I put his harness on him, tightened it a bit, then grabbed my water bottle, and headed downstairs. My mind spun over the paper clipped note, Dead Words. I found myself walking in the direction of Shoetown.

Maybe it was serendipity. I could see the words for myself again. Still, it was a bit creepy when I found myself in front of the building, and it was taped off as a crime scene. I knew the police had been there, and wondered what they had found.

I glanced down the street where we'd met that boy, Billy. Curious, I walked back that way to his house. I doubted he'd even be home, but I thought it might be a good idea to check. Maybe, without my aunt squawking about police, he might have more to say.

The stairs were every bit as rickety as the first time we'd been there. This time, there was a car in the driveway. The screen door screeched when I opened it to knock on the front door.

Footsteps echoed inside. I juggled Shakespeare and gave him a kiss on his head while I waited.

The door opened, and a youngish woman stood there. Her face wore a guarded expression. "Hello? Can I help you?"

"Hello. Sorry to bother you. My aunt and I were walking by here the other day, and a boy from this house offered us an iced tea. I just wanted to thank you." A thought came to me, and I opened my purse. "And to give him this. As a special thank you. He really helped my aunt." I held out a twenty dollar bill.

She glanced at it, and her eyes widened. Slowly, she took it. "That's my son. He's got the kindest heart. Where he got it from, I don't know." Then she yelled over her shoulder, "Billy!"

There were thundering footsteps, then the kid from earlier skidded around the corner. He came to a stop when he saw me and stared up at his mom.

"This nice lady wanted to reward you for giving them iced tea." The mom gestured to me.

Billy walked forward. "Oh, yeah! I remember you!" He reached out to pet Shakespeare. "And your cat too. Where's that funny old woman?"

"Billy!" His mom gasped, shocked.

I laughed. "She'd probably agree it's true. She's home resting."

"After you came that day, the police showed up."

"At your house?"

"No. Over there." He pointed to the factory then bit his lip. "Where I saw those people."

That's what I wanted. "Oh, yes. Can you tell me about them at all?"

"I guess I can now, since the police already know. It was two men. One was real drunk."

Billy's mom rolled her eyes.

"What?" the boy asked. "He was. He fell down by the dumpster over there and pulled the other guy down as well. The second guy had a heck of a time picking him back up."

"Then what happened?" I asked.

"He dragged him inside that building."

"Can you tell me what happened next?"

He shook his head adamantly. "No. Mom came in then and told me to get back in bed."

"So, it was early in the morning?"

"Yeah. Still dark out."

I glanced over. "How could you see, then?"

"There's that street light right there." He pointed down the sidewalk. "Shines right over there."

"Did you tell the police any of this?"

It seemed Billy's mom had had enough. "All right. Back inside," she told the boy. She looked at me. "And thank you for this. We can use it." With that, she leaned past me and grabbed the screen door. I stepped back so she could shut it, which she did without acknowledging me again.

I went back down the steps as the front door closed behind me with a resounding thud.

"That went well," I whispered into Shakespeare's fur.

Back on the sidewalk, I eyed the abandoned factory again. Then I headed over.

The yellow caution tape taped to the door fluttered in the breeze. I set the cat down to sniff around a bit while I studied the dumpster.

Gently, I gave the leash a little tug, "Come on, buddy."

We walked over there, while I checked out the ground around the dumpster. I could see a scrape mark from when the men fell. I squatted down to take a picture, giving Shakespeare more of a lead.

I couldn't make out a footprint, just a scuff. Honestly, I couldn't even be certain it wasn't made by the police going in and out.

I stood back and stared at the door.

Shakespeare gave one of his special meows, calling my attention.

"I don't have any snacks with me," I said absentmindedly, as I ran my gaze around the area in front of the door. I didn't see blood or any sign of struggle.

He tugged on the leash, making me turn toward him.

"What is it, buddy?"

He was furiously pawing at something in the thin layer of gravel beneath the dumpster. It moved out of his reach, so he lay on his side and dug, like it was one of his toys trapped under the sofa.

I bent down to see. "What did you find?" I saw a shiny thing and reached for a tissue in my pocket. Carefully, I wiggled the shiny object from beneath the dumpster wheel. Shakespeare mewed as I extracted it and stood to sniff what I'd found.

It was a key. Not a large key, such as you would put into a doorknob, nor was it too small. It wasn't the type to fit into a padlock. I knew I recognized it from somewhere. Frowning, I wrapped the key in the tissue and placed it in my pocket. My heart began to race. I had the distinct impression that I may have literally found the key to the entire case.

I called to Shakespeare; he readily leaped into my arms.

As I walked home with Shakespeare, I heard something behind me. Something that said, "Bad news."

Something that said, "Run."

Chapter Thirteen

Cautiously, I glanced over my shoulder, my heart sinking like a stone as I spotted a group of young hoodlums emerge from the shadowy alleyway like characters from a noir film. They wasted no time, their lanky forms quickly cutting through the dim light towards me.

One of them, with a sneer that could curdle milk, called out something, though the words were lost in their laughter. A wave of menace electrified the air, making the hairs on the back of my neck stand at attention.

I clutched my coat closer, feeling for the reassuring outline of my keychain in my pocket—a makeshift weapon if things got too dicey.

The only sounds on the street were the soft patter of my feet and their heavier, more determined steps. I knew I had to think fast. These weren't the kind of kids you'd find at a bake sale. They had the look of trouble.

They called again, and I heard their footsteps speed up. I didn't wait around to find out what those kids wanted from me. Clutching Shakespeare, I dashed off in the opposite direction with the cat bouncing like a furry basketball in my arms.

I have to admit, it had been a while since I'd done anything more strenuous than channel surfing. In a bizarre twist of fate, Aunt Mattie's voice echoed in my ears, giving me an impromptu lecture on the benefits of cardio. The street was as empty as my fridge on a Sunday night, so our mad dash went unnoticed. My breath came in short gasps, and my legs felt like they were about to go on strike. But the sound of their footsteps behind me was like an extra shot of espresso.

Finally, I stumbled into a park where some people were gathered, looking like they'd never seen a woman run for her life with a cat before. Maybe, just maybe, these folks could serve as my unwitting guardians. I slowed down, just enough to suck in some air like I was trying to inflate a balloon.

"Sorry, Shakespeare," I wheezed, "I didn't sign up for the feline 5K."

Thankfully, we eventually made it home without incident. My nerves were frayed, and it took hours for the adrenaline to dissipate and for my heart to stop racing like it was in a marathon. In hindsight, though, this experience gave me some good lessons—the main one being don't visit a murder scene without keeping an extra special eye out!

An odd thing happened after all that petrifying fear subsided; hunger grabbed me with an intensity that matched the fear I'd just experienced. I found myself in the kitchen, assembling the comforting simplicity of a BLT.

The crunch of the bacon, the freshness of the lettuce, and the ripe tomato made one of the best meals I'd ever had. Who knew being afraid for your life was such a flavor intensifier? I poured myself a tall glass of milk and took a big gulp.

Shakespeare, who had been my unwilling accomplice in this escapade, appeared equally ravenous. He watched me and his whiskers twitched in anticipation.

"Okay, just one piece," I said and handed him a piece of bacon. Carefully, he took it, and purred with gratitude, and gave my hand a head bump.

As we ate, the silence of the house was now comforting. Afterward, I found two cookies remaining in a package in the cupboard and finished them off with the last of the milk.

It was odd how the fear made me even more anxious to solve the crime. It had even turned into a strange emotion, like it was me against "them," and I was determined to win. It made me think how often I'd chided Aunt Mattie about getting involved in such things, but now, maybe I could understand it.

Hunger satisfied, I walked over to my computer and settled into the swivel chair. I'd spent so many hours in that chair that it had my bodily imprint on it. Shakespeare jumped up onto the table where I'd put a little cat bed. It was either that or he would try to sleep on the keyboard.

I think he liked the sound of the clicking keys. And whenever I made a sound when I was pleased with what I'd written, he'd look up and give me a cat smile.

I sure loved this cat. Rescuing him turned out to be the best thing that had ever happened to me. Our friendship had grown stronger with each passing day. He was now my best friend too. His presence kept me grounded even when the world seemed ready to spin off its axis, and for that, I will be eternally grateful.

Chapter Fourteen

The first thing I did on the computer was to navigate to the website where my own blogs appeared. I knew the site only had one ongoing blog, and I assumed that the company had decided to hire other bloggers for perspective and perhaps to fill in the gaps when I was off solving mysteries with my aunt. I clicked through the posts until I found one I hadn't written. Sure enough, the author was David Porter.

It read: "Welcome to the Whiskers Cat Food blog! We're so excited to talk to you about all things cats and cat food."

His article continued on about several nutritional needs of cats. Very humdrum stuff. However, I finally had a picture of him.

It was only thumbnail in size, but it rested just above his byline. I had to zoom in repeatedly to enlarge it, but there was no doubt. That was the poor man we'd seen the other morning.

I wasn't sure if seeing him alive and well brought me relief, or even more sadness. But regardless of my own emotions, his killer was still on the loose.

What would be someone's motive to kill him? A chill ran down my arm. Could it be something that could be transferred to me? I made up my mind that I would never go down to the warehouse again, unless there was an officer with me. I couldn't take the risk. After all, if something happened to me, where would Shakespeare go?

I slid my hand into my pocket and pulled out the small tissue that contained the key. Again, it looked familiar to me. Quickly, I dug into the search engine to do a search for images of keys.

Pages upon pages of them rolled past me as I scrolled downward. That turned out to be a dead end. There were just too many options.

Still determined, I opened my drawer and pulled out a magnifying glass. Carefully, I situated the key to look for any identifying marks. Not seeing any, I flipped it over and turned on the desk lamp.

There were four numbers on one side in tiny print.

Excitement flickered inside my stomach. I pulled out a sheet of note paper and noted the numbers. The excitement seemed ungrounded since I couldn't prove it had belonged to David. However, I had found it where David had fallen, and it didn't look like it had been there long.

I remembered the to-go coffee cup. Aunt Mattie had jotted the name down. Where was that paper?

I ran to the laundry and pulled out my pants. There stuffed in the pocket was the crumpled paper. Quickly, I smoothed it flat and scrolled the testimony. That's it! I ran back, feeling sweaty, and typed it in.

Sure enough, there was a coffee bar with that name. Even better, it was in our very town. With a smile, I jotted down the address. There's one thing!

With some trepidation, I picked up the phone and tapped out Aunt Mattie's number.

"Hello?"

"It's me."

"I know it's you. I've been waiting all day for this phone call, and you know how I hate to wait! How did the office visit go?" she added impatiently.

"It was kind of a bust. And then Shakespeare and I took a walk." I shifted in my chair, my index finger sliding into the collar of my blouse. I didn't want to tell her the little detail about getting chased.

"I can hear in your voice something happened. Don't keep anything from me, my girl. You know I will find out one way or another."

I decided to deflect. "Interesting you say that. I noticed that you haven't asked about my date with Officer Timothy. Could that be because you've already been on the phone to him?"

"Oh. He told you?" She inadvertently convicted herself with that response.

"Yep. Just a wee bit embarrassing, you know."

"Oh, girlie. I'm your only living relative. There's no one but me to look out for you, so of course I'm going to interrogate a strange man taking you out. I'm not shy about that!"

I laughed. "No, you certainly are not shy."

"I'm glad that's settled. Now, hurry, dearie. I'm not getting any younger. What have you found out?"

"You know, Aunt Mattie, you are constantly pestering me to be more like you. So, you'll be proud I'm doing it now."

"Oh! Being brave!" She sounded proud.

"Yeah, brave. Bravely poking my nose into other people's business."

"Emily!" she gasped.

I laughed again. "I'm just teasing you. Listen, I'd really like to look at those pictures again. Can you find them?"

"Hold on."

I waited, swiveling around to pet Shakespeare, whose tail curled lazily over his back with pleasure.

"Okay, I found them. What is it you're looking for?"

The problem was, I wasn't certain what it was either. It was just a feeling that I had overlooked something. "I'll give you this instead. I know you want to know that my date went very well, and I would like to see him again."

Aunt Mattie chuckled, "Well, that's the best news I've heard all day! Now, are you tell me what's going on?"

I decided I didn't want to talk about it on the phone. "Can you come over tomorrow? We can look over the photos together."

"I'm getting my hair rinsed in the morning."

I grinned. That was what she called coloring it, because it didn't sound as permanent.

She quickly added, "When I'm done, I'll come by."

"Perfect," I said. We said our goodbyes, and I turned back to the Whisker Treats blog. It made me realize I needed to talk to more people who knew him.

Soon, I was pouring over every available record I could find on the internet about David. I searched through his social media, through the white pages, and even paid for one of those silly background checks. The more I did, the more I learned about the man whose body we'd found.

Then I came to the one page that trumped all the rest. It was, perhaps, the single biggest clue in the entire mystery.

In searching for his name, and the town where he lived, I came across an obituary. He was mentioned as a survivor to the deceased. The deceased was none other than Mark Porter —the twin brother of David.

Chapter Fifteen

I knew I had to visit Whisker Treats again. The next morning, with a mix of reluctance and determination, I got myself ready to head back. It was ironic, really; I'd now visited my job site more this week than I had in the last two years I'd worked there. But it had to be done. I needed to speak to some of my co-workers during their lunch break, hoping to uncover more about the mystery at hand.

Naturally, my favorite lady, Sheila, was working once again. She greeted me with her usual glare but didn't ask why I was there, and I didn't volunteer the information. She would find out soon enough, no doubt through the office grapevine.

I made my way through to the back where there was an eating area, a cozy nook filled with the chatter and clinking of cutlery from the employees enjoying their lunch. There was even a cute little cafeteria at Whisker Treats, complete with mismatched tables and chairs, and posters of cats adorning the walls.

As I walked in, it felt like everyone was staring at me, though I knew that was probably just my imagination playing tricks. I was, after all, not a common sight around here these days.

I stopped at each table, scanning faces for David's co-workers. The first person I had a chance to talk to was Lisa, a young woman with bright eyes and an even brighter smile, who worked at the advertising desk.

"Sorry to bother you, but I wanted to see if you knew David Porter?"

She looked up from her salad, her tone guarded. "Do I know you?"

"I'm one of the blog writers here. You're Lisa, right?" I asked, trying to sound casual. "Mind if I sit for a moment?"

She nodded, her eyes widening slightly with curiosity. "Sure," she gestured to the empty chair. "So, you're one of the lucky ones that gets to work at home."

I nodded, almost feeling as if I needed to apologize for my job.

"I don't think I would get a lick of work done if I had to stay home. My three-year-old climbs on me like I'm play equipment."

We both shared a smile. "So, what's this about David?"

I took a breath, knowing this conversation could go in many directions. "I was wondering if you've noticed anything unusual around here lately, especially with David?"

She picked at her salad. "I know David just as an acquaintance. However, he was always friendly with everyone, and always willing to help out when needed." She leaned in, lowering her voice as if sharing a secret. "And he always had plenty of money."

I thought of his fancy shoes. "So, was he rich?"

"He sure seemed like it. I tried to get him to ask me out, but he never did," she gave a regretful sigh.

I wasn't sure what to think about that. "Thank you for your time," I said as I stood.

She brightened up. "Hey, you should talk to Gary. They were actual friends. I think he got him a job here."

"Really?"

She pointed to a man sitting at another table. I recognized him right away. He was a quiet, bespectacled man with an air of meticulousness that only an accountant could possess. He'd been with Whisker Treats longer than most. I approached his table where he was organizing his lunch tray, each item placed with precision.

"Gary, do you mind if I join you for a moment?"

He looked up, a little surprised but nodded. "Emily, isn't it? Of course, sit down."

I pulled out a chair, and after a brief exchange of pleasantries, I got to the point. "I'm so sorry about David. I just heard."

Gary's expression softened at the mention of David's name. "Yes, tragic, really. We used to have lunch together quite often. He was always a good listener, and I could trust him with confidential matters."

"Did he ever mention anything odd or out of the ordinary lately?" I pressed gently, aware that I was treading on the personal.

Gary shook his head slowly. "Not that I recall. But there was this one time, just a couple of weeks before... well, before he was no longer here. He seemed a bit distracted, kept checking his phone. I asked if everything was okay, but he just said he was dealing with some personal stuff, nothing to worry about."

I nodded, making a mental note. David's distracted behavior might not have been significant to Gary at the time, but every detail mattered.

"Thank you," I said, standing up. "I appreciate you sharing that."

"If there's anything else I can help with, let me know. David was a good friend."

"Again, I'm so sorry."

"Me, too." He gave a small, sad smile.

After speaking with Gary, my next conversation was with Sam, a junior manager with an easy-going demeanor. I approached his table, he greeted me with a nod.

"I see you're making your rounds," he said.

"I just have a few questions. Mind if I join you?" I asked, pulling out a chair.

"Not at all," Sam replied, his eyes curious but friendly. "What brings you here today?"

I got straight to the point. "I'm trying to piece together more about David. Did you know him?"

Sam's face softened. "Yeah, we often went out for drinks after work, David was a great guy to be around." He took a bite of his sandwich, chewing thoughtfully. "Everyone here looked up to him, you know? He had this incredible work ethic, always committed to excellence. He was the kind of person who made you want to do better, not just for yourself but for the team."

I leaned in, curious by the portrait Sam was painting of David. "Did he ever mention anything unusual or concerning in the time leading up to his disappearance?"

Sam paused, his brow furrowing. "Not directly, no. But looking back, there were these subtle changes. He seemed a bit more stressed, maybe a little distracted. I thought it was just work pressure, but maybe there was more to it."

"Did you know anything about his family?" I asked, quietly.

"Not really. He was a loner." He paused, as if trying to pull out a deep memory. "I do recall him saying he lost his brother as a teenager. Poor guy."

I felt my spine stiffen at the confirmation of what I'd found the night before. Swallowing, I nodded. "Thanks, Sam. This has been really helpful," I said, preparing to leave.

"If you find out anything, let us know, yeah? We all want closure," he replied sadly.

At every table I visited, more people told me stories about their relationship with David - some funny anecdotes from around the office, others more serious reflections on what it meant to be his friend or colleague at Whisker Treats. From all these conversations emerged one underlying truth: everyone loved working with him.

The last person I spoke to was Martha, the gal who'd helped me the first time.

She smiled as I approached. "So, you're back, huh? Still have questions?"

I nodded.

"I've heard you talking to everyone. I wish I had more to tell you. Still, it's such a shock, isn't it?"

"It definitely is."

"Whether we knew him well or not, he was one of the Whisker Treats family."

"That's right," I said. I thanked her, feeling like I wanted to give her a hug.

As I left the building, the puzzle seemed to grow both more complicated. David's role in this company, his friendships, and his secrets – they all painted a picture of a man whose life was both a mixture of mystery and tragedy.

Chapter Sixteen

The ding of the street-level bell reverberated through my apartment like a bat signal, announcing Aunt Mattie's arrival.

I buzzed her in, unlocked my door, and flicked the switch on the teapot. In stormed Aunt Mattie, her now newly-rinsed fiery red hair leading the charge like she was about to tackle an obstacle course.

"Wow! I love it!" I exclaimed.

"It suits me, don't you think?"

Shakespeare, spotting her, dove for my room, probably with visions of the cat carrier in his head. Apparently, he wasn't inclined to have another visit at her house any time soon.

"It definitely does." I said. "You ready for some tea? And I have cake today."

"Cake?" Her face lit up like she'd just won the lottery as she plonked her purse down. "I can always use some cake."

I unveiled the fudge cake I'd snagged on my way home and then grabbed a pair of plates and a knife. I set them before her and she made a happy sound. By the time I turned with the tea canister, she'd already carved herself a slice large enough to be considered a national monument.

I pulled out a chair and sat as she took a bite.

"This place has really come together," she mused, savoring her cake like it was her last meal. "It feels like you."

I looked up, stunned. Aunt Mattie wasn't exactly known for dishing out compliments. I knew if she peeked behind that bedroom door, I'd be in for a lecture on clutter management.

"Thanks, Aunt Mattie. I've been working on it. It's nice to have a space that's just mine." I poured the hot water, watching the tea leaves do their magic.

She nodded, her stern gaze softening. "You know, I always look forward to our tea times and chats." Another bite, another moment of bliss. "And you have the best snacks."

I chuckled. "Glad you like them."

"So, what's your next step?"

"I'm going to check out the coffee shop. You know, from the cup we found?"

She chased a crumb and squashed it with the back of her fork.

"Have you talked with Brandon yet? Excuse me, Officer Timothy."

Despite my longing to involve Brandon, I hesitated, aware that involving him could strain our budding relationship.

"You mean about the case?"

"I was just wondering if he let anything slip yet."

I shook my head and took a bite. "Not yet."

"I'm surprised they haven't given an official statement yet about the poor man."

My fork froze halfway to my mouth. "What do you mean?"

"I mean they haven't publicly identified the body yet."

"What? Of course they have. People know about it."

"Well, I'm sure his family knows. As for everyone else, rumors, I suppose. It is a small town." She licked the bit of extra frosting off her fork.

Shakespeare must have decided it was safe. Either that, or his stomach overruled because he snuck out of the bedroom to watch us. After watching us for a moment, he casually made his way over, stopping for a moment for an emergency cat itch that had to be licked. He ended that with a huge lion yawn that ended in a yowl. He thought he was being cute when he did that and expected to be rewarded with a cake crumb.

Of course, I did it right away.

Aunt Mattie adjusted her glasses to watch. "That cat's going to need more walks if you keep that up."

I was more interested in the gold cylinder on a chain around her neck. "Is that your miniature kaleidoscope?"

"Of course it is." She pulled it up to peep through it, spinning it slightly. "Now, are you ready to look at the photos?"

"Did you bring the prints?"

"Not this time, but you could look on my phone."

She didn't wait for my answer but rummaged through her purse, the sound of keys jangling. "Now, where did I put that thing?" she muttered to herself, finally pulling out the sleek device with a triumphant smile. "Here it is," she said, handing it over to me. "You know how to use it?"

I tried not to smile as I nodded and accepted her phone.

Slowly, I found her photos and scrolled through them, pausing at the shot of the scrawled out, 'Dead Words'.

That phrase bothered me. What did that mean? While I pondered that, I flipped through the ones she'd taken of the items in his wallet.

Suddenly, I froze. There was one of a scrap of paper she'd found in the billfold. It had numbers scrawled on it. I jumped up and ran for my desk, quickly rifling through the drawer until I found the paper I'd recorded the numbers I'd found on the key. Hurrying back, I compared the two.

A perfect match. My heart pounded. The key I found was his key! I knew it!

Now I just had to figure out what it went to. And why would he have the numbers from the key written down and saved in his wallet?

Of course, Aunt Mattie watched all this with a suspicious stare. "Are you going to tell me why you're running around like a jackrabbit, or just keep it a secret?"

"Look at this!" I showed her the picture and the paper. "I found this key by the dumpster the other day."

She took it, interested, and pulled up her readers. "You went back, hmm? After you told me how dangerous it was?"

I blustered through her question with one of my own. "What do you think it belongs to? A post office box?"

"I have no idea," I said, bewildered. I continued to scroll through the pictures, stopping on the coffee cup.

"Here's my next step." I shoved my phone over to display the coffee shop's web page. "It's where the cup came from."

"Dutch Cup! I've been there before. They have good biscotti. You want me to tag along?"

I shook my head. This needed to be handled with finesse, not with a jackhammer. "No. I have to do some errands afterward."

"I know this is like swallowing a cactus for you, Emily," she started, her voice dripping with the kind of sympathy that could only come from someone who's watched too many soap operas, "but we're stuck in this mess together. Let's team up like Batman and Robin, minus the tights."

Laughing, I wrapped her in a hug and gave her a good squeeze. "When I've got the scoop, I swear I'll ring you up." I took a sip of tea. "You think his family does know?"

"They notify the next of kin right away. Identify the body and such."

I cringed and grabbed my phone again. "That make me think...."

"What's that?"

"I want to look into more about Daniel. That's David's twin brother. He died when they were teenagers."

"You think it's linked?" she asked. Shakespeare came over to rub against her legs. She snagged another crumb and lowered her hand to him. As I watched, her eyes widened, daring me to say anything.

It wasn't worth it, despite her scolding me earlier. "I'm not sure. But his friend from work mentioned it. And that post his sister made...."

"What part?"

"Where she said she couldn't believe it happened again."

"You have that thing happening again," Aunt Mattie said. "Stop it."

"Stop what?"

Those lines forming on your forehead. You keep doing that face and you'll make it permanent."

I rubbed my forehead. She used to tell me that as a child when I crossed my eyes. "It's my thinking face."

"Good heavens, child. Eat a bite of cake. No one can make that kind of face while enjoying this chocolate delight."

I did as she said as I scrolled. I found the obituary headline I'd discovered the other night but there was no more information. Chewing and musing, I started typing some more.

After a few minutes of quiet, I shouted, "Bingo!"

The fork clattered in the plate as Aunt Mattie jumped. "Emily Lickinson! You warn a person before you do that." Then curiosity grabbed her. "What did you find?"

"His name led to a town's newspaper archive." Clearing my throat, I read it out loud. "In a heartrending revelation, Daniel Porter's mother spoke about the loss of her son in the quiet town of Millfield. Daniel died of a drug overdose in an alley near their old home, a case still open. A victim of what some believe is a first time drug-use, his death comes as a warning to those who want to experiment. Ellen, his mother, shared with us through tears, Daniels's love for rock-climbing and his hope for college . His twin brother, David, denied that his brother used drugs, and swore he would try to get justice for his brother. David was starting college this year in place of his brother, to pursue a career in journalism."

"My goodness! Another tragic death! That poor family!"

I set my fork down. I no longer had an appetite. "It's strange everyone thinks David died from a drug overdose as well."

"The police keep those kinds of details private during the investigation, I'm sure."

"You think that David found his brother's killer?"

"After all these years?'

I nodded. "And that's what led to his own murder."

Whoever I was dealing with, they weren't to be taken lightly. They were capable of vengeance and had dangerous secrets they were hiding.

Moreover, I couldn't let Aunt Mattie anywhere near the investigation. They would kill her.

They might kill me.

Chapter Seventeen

The coffee shop was a bit of a drive, right in the heart of town. I never loved coming down here because parking was so hard to find. And I'd rather drive around forever than parallel park.

Finally, I found a spot at an antique store just down the street. Just as I was about to get out, my cell rang. I checked it and butterflies began when I saw it was from Brandon.

"Hey, Brandon!" I said, trying to sound casual."

"Em! Long time no talk. I just wanted to check in. How are you?"

My heart smiled to hear him give me a nickname. Then I looked at the coffee shop and swallowed. "Oh, nothing. Just hanging out. How's your day going?"

"Typical. Paperwork and patrol. Boring."

I chuckled. "Oh, come on. It can't be that bad."

"But I'm glad I got to hear your voice. Where you hanging out at?"

I swallowed again. "I'm actually about to get a coffee, then go home and write. That's about it."

"Sounds like you're living the dream."

We did a few more rounds with the smalltalk and then he had to go. But not before he asked if I was free this weekend.

My heart was light when I hung up, and I'm sure I had a stupid grin on my face. I tried to compose myself as I got out and locked the door. The wind picked up and blew my hair around, making me feel like I carried a tumbleweed on my head.

I hurried down the sidewalk and pushed open the Dutch Cup door. Above me, a little chime from a bell signaled my entry. The scent of roasted beans and fresh pastry enveloped me.. I inhaled deeply as I tried to smooth down my hair.

The place was buzzing with an afternoon rush. I glanced around, wondering if it would be worth showing David's photo to the other customers. Several were furiously typing behind laptops, and one had on headphones. And what if I found a friend of his? Would they know he had died?

The thought of that bothered me for more than one reason. As it came to me, the hair on my arms rose. How did my co-workers know David was gone without an official word? Was someone in contact with his parents?

Shrugging it off, I decided to start my detective work with the barista, hoping she had a knack for details and a memory for faces. After glancing around, I spotted her wrestling with an espresso machine. She sported short blonde hair and a grin that could light up Millfield's gloomiest day.

"Hello! What can I get started for you today?" she chirped.

I sidled up to the counter. "How about a chai tea?" I asked.

She rattled off the sizes like she was auctioning off livestock, and I went for a small. As I fumbled with my debit card, I also whipped out my phone.

"Actually, I'm on a bit of a hunt," I confessed, swiping to David's photo, his smile as broad as the town's Main Street. "Have you seen this guy?" I slid the phone towards her.

The barista peered at the screen. "Yeah, I remember him. Came in a couple of days ago. Super nice, but he seemed like he was late for his own funeral."

My pulse did a little tap dance. "Do you know where he dashed off to after his coffee?"

She paused, her brows knitting together in thought. "Let me think... Yeah, I remember now. After he left, he went over there." She pointed out the large display window towards the bank on the opposite corner of the street.

A bank? As the barista made my tea, my mind raced through possibilities. Was he withdrawing money, or perhaps meeting someone there?

As I stared at the bank, it dawned on me why the little key had looked so familiar. I had been to that very bank. Years ago, my mom had left me one when she had died, going to a security box.

There hadn't been much in the security box, just her marriage certificate and a few other sentimental things. I'd left them there so as not to lose them through my many moves.

Panic hit me as I realized I wasn't sure where I'd stashed the key.

The barista came back with the cup and rang me up. I gave her a tip, trying to control my excitement. "Thanks, Lisa. You've been a huge help."

"Anytime. I hope you find him," the barista replied with genuine concern.

With a new lead in hand, I exited the coffee shop, my gaze fixed on the bank across the street. I considered my next move. The bank loomed before me, not just as a building, but as a beacon of hope.

One I hoped would not turn out to be a dead end.

But first, I needed to get home and find my key. I hoped I hadn't lost it.

Chapter Eighteen

The urgency of my mission propelled me through the door of my apartment, my mind set on one singular goal—find my key to the security box. I tossed my jacket onto the back of a chair, the table still cluttered with cake plates and empty mugs.

Now, where would I have put it?

I pulled out a few junk drawers, even the utensil drawer. But I knew it wasn't there. Frustrated, I pushed back my hair and tried to think.

Shakespeare darted between my legs, meowing plaintively, tail flicking with impatience.

"Not now, buddy," I muttered, stepping over him carefully as I made my way to my bedroom. Shakespeare, undeterred, followed, weaving around my ankles like a furry, purring obstacle.

In my bedroom, I went straight for my sock drawer. I yanked it open, socks of various colors and states of matching tumbling out. I dug through them, tossing pairs over my shoulder, but no key. Shakespeare, seeing this as an impromptu play session, pounced on a particularly fluffy sock, dragging it under the bed with triumphant meows.

"Great, just great," I sighed, watching him play. I looked through the drawer again, and then shoved it closed with a thud. I turned to the closet, where boxes of unpacked belongings lay stacked.

There was nothing for it. I had to search through them. I pulled the first one down, the dust making me sneeze. Old books, and a box of photographs from college came out, but no key. It was hard not to get lost in the nostalgia, but I shoved the box closed and grabbed a new one. This one held holiday decorations.

Shakespeare, now bored with the sock, decided the boxes were his new playground. He jumped into the first one and settled down, watching me with curious green eyes.

"Shakespeare, are you trying to help?" I asked, gently lifting him out. He immediately leaped back in as soon as I turned away. I covered my face, trying to think as my frustration grew.

The key had to be here, somewhere. I knew I wouldn't have thrown it away. My memory raced through my move here. Where would I have put it? I promised myself at the time to keep it safe.

I squashed down a fearful imagination of boxes tossed in the dumpster, along with the words, "What if...."

Panicked, I kept digging. Finally, in the very last box, hidden beneath a pile of old concert tickets, my fingers brushed against a small wooden jewelry box. I pulled it out and opened it. I nearly cried as I pulled out the small, unassuming key. I turned it over to see its silver surface slightly tarnished but inscribed with four numbers.

"Gotcha!" I exclaimed, relief washing over me. I settled back on my heels while Shakespeare, sensing my excitement, began purring loudly as if to congratulate me.

No time to enjoy the relief. I sprang to my feet in search for the key I found at the dumpster. They were a perfect match.

With the key in hand, I gave Shakespeare a quick pet, whispering, "I promise, once this is over, we'll have all the time for cuddles."

I stared at the strewn boxes and clothes. "And now it's time to dress. Dress to impress."

I had a job to do.

Chapter Nineteen

The afternoon was ticking away, but I still had time to get back to the bank. I looked at myself in the mirror, picked out a dust bunny from my hair, and then applied some lipstick. After scrutinizing myself again, I shrugged and grabbed my purse. Then, locking the door, and running to my car, I prepared myself for the ordeal ahead.

The main thing on my mind was hoping not to get arrested.

The parking spot in front of the antique store was taken, but I found a free spot on the other side of the bank. I took a sip of the now cold chai tea to steady myself. After a few more deep breaths, and checking for the keys, I locked the car door.

Inside, the bank was a hive of activity. People moved about, and there was the muted sound of chatter and the clacking of keyboards.

Boldly, I approached one of the tellers to ask for assistance with the safety deposit boxes. After a brief wait, a banker named Mr. Henderson, with a neatly trimmed beard and kind eyes, led me through a secure door that led to the room where they kept the security boxes. He checked my identification, then used his key to open the door.

The air was cooler in here, the walls lined with rows upon rows of metal security boxes. Mr. Henderson watched me open the outer lock of my box, number 4531.

Once the box was unlocked, Mr. Henderson gave me a reassuring nod. "All right, then. I'll leave you to it, Miss Lickenson. Take your time. Just buzz when you're done," he said. He then stepped away, leaving me alone in the dimly lit room.

I watched him leave as my inner mind question if I really was going to do this. When the door shut tight, I spun around to look for 3232. Finding it, I quickly opened David's box, my heart racing with each second.

I raised the lid slowly with my heart beating like a drum solo to a heavy metal band. I thought it was empty at first, and then I shook the box. In the back was a small notebook whose cover was worn from use, and an old cassette tape. I had to believe these were the clues to David's fate. I grabbed them both and stuffed them into my purse, and then relocked his box.

Sweat sprung on my forehead. Breathing deeply to calm myself and force myself to slow down, I rummaged through the contents of my box. My heart squeezed to see a picture of my mom and dad on their wedding day. After a moment of hesitation, I stuck that in my purse as well. Then I locked mine.

Taking another second to wipe my forehead and tidy my hair, I pushed the button for the buzzer. The door opened and I firmly walked out.

"Thank you so much for your help," I said as I passed Mr. Henderson, my voice steady despite the adrenaline.

"Take care, and come back if you need anything else," he called after me.

Back in the safety of my apartment, I leaned against the locked door, exhaling deeply. Finally, I felt safe. In my purse the notebook filled with cryptic notes. My heart pounded not just from the close call but from the realization that the web surrounding David was far more intricate than I had imagined.

As I surveyed the kitchen, with all its opened drawers and strewn content, I started shaking. The effects of adrenaline had hit me. I sat in a chair for a moment to try to pull myself together. Then I made myself a cup of coffee. While it was brewing, I opened the cake box and got a fork, and took bites right out of the cake.

Shakespeare came around the corner, dragging the before mentioned sock. Not so fuzzy now, it looked well-loved, with a hole in the toe.

"You can have it," I said and got my coffee mug. Then I opened my purse.

The first thing to come out was the picture of my parents. I smiled as I looked at it, then looked around the house for a place to put it. My gaze landed on my one framed picture next to the TV, the photo inside of me receiving my first writing award. I grabbed the frame, wiped the dust of the top off on my pants, and carefully removed the picture. Gently, I put in the one of my parents and set it back on the TV stand. Memories filled me as I stared.

I gave the frame a little nudge to straighten it more, then went back to my purse.

With my mug in hand, along with the little notebook, I headed to my room. I froze in the doorway, having forgotten about the tornado I'd unleashed in there earlier. Even worse, it appeared that Shakespeare had done some damage as well when I'd left.

I couldn't think about that now. I shoved aside the tangled heap of clothes on the bed, creating a small empty spot. Then, both excited and nervous, I settled in with the journal on my lap.

It was time to dive into its secrets.

Shakespeare apparently wanted to know as well, and leapt onto the bed. I gave him an absent-minded head scratch and opened the notebook. As I read the first page, I suddenly knew how my co-workers at the Whiskers cat food place knew that David Porter had died.

Chapter Twenty

That evening, I read through the journal two more times, my eyes tracing over each line, each word. I glanced at the cassette tape resting against my parent's picture, but I had no way to play it. One problem at a time.

One passage in the middle of the notebook especially stood out to me.

"Got another ten thousand from him today. He calls it dead words, what I'm doing. Sounds better than blackmail, I guess. But accident or not, he ruined my parents' life. He ruined mine as well, and he took my brother's. And he knows I have proof. He didn't know he left it when he left my brother to die. I don't know what his problem is, anyway. It's not like it's his money."

I went back to the opening pages of the book, compelled by a need to understand the narrative from the very start. There, in the stark black ink on the yellowed paper, was the assertion that shook the foundation of the story.

David wrote, "They say my brother died of a drug overdose. But I know Daniel didn't do drugs. He used to say he'd break my leg if he ever caught me doing it."

This declaration painted a vivid picture of Daniel's character, one of protective sternness and a zero-tolerance policy towards drugs. It immediately went against the news story that he had died of drug overdose.

Over all, I'd say David's handwriting was on the messier side of neat. I could read it, but a few of the words I had to look at for a moment. So it was strange that the last few pages of the notebook were meticulously designed to resemble an old-fashioned ledger. It featured columns and rows, that were all neatly filled with numbers. The handwriting was precise, suggesting the importance of every single figure listed.

Each number equaled a years worth of my salary.

I thought about his paystub I found in his the file. I remember reading the amount and glossing over it because I thought he was hired to be paid yearly, with advances. Kind of like a book author.

So I was quite shocked to see that all these numbers were monthly amounts.

Slowly I scanned the page. The accounting went back years. I turned the page and continued on. The older the year the lower the money amount was. In the beginning, there was one payout per year.

And the first payment was a few months after Daniel's death. This one had a simple note. "G owes me, and I'm going to make him pay."

I stood at the crossroads of decision, feeling the weight of my potential next move. I knew I could flush out the murderer, just as David had done. All it would take was an article, cleverly constructed to bait the killer into a response. And I knew he would respond.

But the big question loomed over me—should I write the article? By doing so, I might endanger myself and others, yet the chance to bring justice and closure to Porter family was tantalizing.

Should I do it?

I sat at my desk, my fingers hovering above over the keyboard. I glanced at the notebook again, where a line jumped out at me.

That did it. I started to type. I wrote quickly, in a questioning style. What happens when there are two suspicious deaths, both of overdose? What kind of cover-up happened that demands to be unraveled? In the quiet town of Millfield, first came the death of Daniel, a young man with no history of substance abuse, his body found in an alley with a needle still in his arm. The coroner's report was swift to conclude it as an accidental overdose, but whispers of disbelief ran through the community.

Then, years later, his twin brother, David, suffered the same fate, found in eerily similar circumstances. What kind of cover-up happened that demands to be unraveled?

It's time for there to be an end of Dead Words.

I read it again, changed a few words, but over all kept it the same. It was just the bait I needed. I knew he'd bite.

For the next step, I created a new, untraceable email account and emailed him the post. My subject line said, "You interested in dead words?"

Satisfied, I waited. I knew he would respond soon. Still, I was surprise when I got up to refill my coffee and my email dinged.

His had immediately responded. I wasn't sure if he'd even had time to read through what I wrote. It was a simple sentence. "Who are you?"

I answered with confidence, "I've got the proof you want."

He wrote back, "How much?"

Again, surprise hit me that he'd be so bold. I typed back, playing my cards close, "How much did you give before?"

His reply was sharp, "You're bluffing."

"Let's meet and you can find out."

"Where?"

I knew just the spot. "Dutch Cup."

"Tomorrow at noon. Come alone."

The realization hit me like a ton of bricks. It was true, everything I thought had been true. David had been extracting money from someone at the Whiskers Cat Food Company.

I wasn't afraid to meet him. He was small and unassuming. Heck, he was even injured. He had to use a crutch.

The only problem with that was, like a wounded animal, did it make him more dangerous?

This was a game of cat and mouse, and I was determined to be the cat. With the evidence in hand, I prepared for the next move in this deadly game of chess.

Now I needed to get a cassette player right away. But where?

Then I knew. Aunt Mattie. She had to have one. She had everything.

Chapter Twenty-One

I was taken aback at how speedily Aunt Mattie arrived once she got the phone call. But, in hindsight, I shouldn't have been surprised; after all, she had a sixth sense for drama.

Clutching the antique tape-recorder like it was the queen's diamond, she burst into the room, her wild, red curls flying. "Spill it, Emily!" she demanded, her eyes wide with a mix of excitement and impatience. "What's this about before I hand over this relic?"

I quickly outlined the situation, my words tumbling out in a rush. "Okay, so there's this security box at the bank where I found this tape," I pointed at the device in her hands, "and a journal. It's all connected to David Porter's murder."

Aunt Mattie's eyebrows shot up, her sarcasm already at full throttle. "Oh, just a tape and a journal. When were you going to tell me?"

"Well, right now, I guess." I pulled out her kryptonite. "Want some pizza? I just had some delivered."

She paused, her eyebrows still lifted in hurt that I'd left her out. Then she spotted the cardboard pizza box. "Well, I might as well just have a bite."

After she got her piece, I settled her down, and then seized the tape player. Carefully, I inserted the tape and pressed play.

"You're the first to hear it," I said, hoping to pacify her.

"Only because you didn't have the equipment," she said before picking an olive off her bosom.

The tape crackled with static. Then I heard a man speaking. "This is David Porter, leaving a confession."

I had chills. He was confessing?

"I've never felt good about what I did. I wanted to make him pay for murdering my brother. The three of us were friends for years. We'd just graduated, and he turned eighteen. Daniel and I got him a Zippo engraved with a G. They went out that night a party but I couldn't go because I was working.

Afterward, G wanted to drive home but Daniel wouldn't let him. They got into an argument which turned into a fight over the keys. Daniel fell backwards and hit his head on a curb. G freaked out, bought a needle full of something, and shot it into him, then dumped him off in the alley.

There was a lot of evidence, including drag marks in the dirt. But once the toxicology report came in, the cops closed the case.

I knew better and went back to look. I found the lighter with my brother, kicked to the side. I heard about the fight from friends at the party. And then I found the dealer who had sold G the drugs.

I should have gone to the police then. But G was scared, and I wanted to do something for my brother. Go to college. So I made G pay. And pay, and pay." The tape stopped here and I was about to eject it. Then it started again with a new recording. "G got this idea to have me work at Whisker Treats Cat Food company. And since he was the accountant, he paid me through their funds. Through his creative accounting. It was no longer his money, but now he was resentful. I told him one last payment and we were done.

He said he would, but he had a look in his eye. Just in case anything goes sideways, I'm leaving this confession." The tape turned into static. I let it play for a bit longer, just to be sure, and then I turned it off.

"Well, isn't that a fine can of worms. I just wished he'd spit out who G was," Aunt Mattie said, irritably.

"I know who he is. I already contacted him."

To say that my aunt's jaw dropped open would be an understatement. You could have fit a cantaloup in there. "Wh-what?" she gasped.

"I did it anonymously. Sent him an email."

She pulled herself together. "And did you sign it with a heart, too?"

I rolled my eyes, knowing she was only half-joking. "I had to do something after I read the journal. David has accounting in there. As soon as he said G, I knew it was Gary from work."

She snorted. "Oh, wonderful, you know him. I hope Gary doesn't want to wipe out someone else because of a good old-fashioned accusation. Is he big?"

"No. In fact, he's injured. I remember Billy saying he saw two men go into the factory. Just before they got through the door, the man he thought was drunk pulled the other man down, injuring him."

"He can use his crutch! He has a weapon!"

Smiling, despite the gravity of the situation, I shook my head.

"No, but that's why I scheduled the meeting at the coffee shop. I thought if he shows up, we'd have the upper hand."

Aunt Mattie looked at the tape recorder with a mock frown. "Emily, I'm a tough old bird. But even I don't think I can take on a killer. Honestly, this was the best idea you could come up with? Luring a murderer out for a cup of coffee? And bringing me for back-up?"

"You do remember you practically shoved me into that dark alley."

"Oh, please, that was just to reminisce about the wishing tree from my youth. I wasn't trying to play cat-and-mouse with a killer," she shot back.

"You always tell me I'm a chip off the old block, and I think this has to be done."

"That's petal off the ol' flower!" She paused, fiddling with her glasses. "I really think you need to call that police officer boyfriend of yours. It's time to get him involved."

"Are you serious?"

"Absolutely. There is only so far we can break the law. Besides, I don't want you dead," she said briskly. "Nor, me either."

I decided she was right. There was no turning back now.

. . .

***

I sent him a text, explaining a few things, to which I received a prompt phone call. It turns out when you say you have some evidence in the latest murder, you get his full attention.

After letting me know he'd be right there, and to try and stay out of trouble in the meantime, he hung up.

Aunt Mattie gave me a pointed look that said, "I told you so," and went to start a fresh pot of coffee.

The scent started to fill my small apartment as I paced nervously by the window, waiting for Brandon.

Moonlight cast long shadows across my eclectic collection of furniture and plants. The security box key sat next to my parent's picture, along with the tape player.

I nervously gnawed on a pizza crust when the buzzer rang. I jumped up and buzzed him, then ran around the apartment, picking things up. Aunt Mattie watched me, shaking her head.

A knock came from the door signaled Brandon's arrival. I opened the door, then stepped back in surprise, not expecting him to still be in uniform. He looked every bit the part of the dedicated police officer he was, and reminded me I may have blurred some legal lines getting this information.

His expression was one of concern mixed with curiosity as he stepped inside, the door closing behind him with a soft click. "Hello, Mattie. Emily," he dipped his head.

"I'm sorry for calling so late. Thanks for coming," I said, feeling both a mixture of relief and stress.

"Of course," he replied, his eyes scanning my face. "You said it was important. Something about evidence into David Porter's death. What's going on?"

Before I could answer, Aunt Mattie hollered from the kitchen, her red hair slightly wilder than usual, "You want some coffee? How about a doughnut?" She gave a little wink.

I winced, thinking, "Not now, auntie!" I decided to ignore my aunt's sarcasm and focus on Brandon. "I found something in a security box. Something that points to who killed David."

Brandon's eyebrows lifted. "The security box? What was in it?"

With a deep breath, I lifted the cassette tape from the table. "This. It was in there with an old notebook. It's David's recording of something important, something he thought was worth hiding away."

Brandon's surprise was evident. He took it from me an looked at it. "I want to ask how you got this, but I have a feeling I better not. From a security box? What's on it?"

"Just listen to it. I thought, with your expertise, we could figure out if it's admissible or if it can even help us."

Aunt Mattie chimed in, "Think of it as a mystery tape from beyond the grave."

Brandon gave her a small smile before turning back to me. "I see you have a player, so I'm assuming you already know what's on it?"

I nodded and pushed the tape player toward him. Carefully, he inserted the tape, the mechanical sounds of the machine filling the silence. The tape began to play, static at first, then David's voice came through, clear but filled with urgency.

The room fell silent as we listened to it, the weight of David's words hanging heavy in the air. Brandon's face hardened with professional resolve. "This is huge, Emily. We need to get this tape to the station, have it analyzed. This could be the key to the case. And reopening his brother's."

Aunt Mattie, sipping her coffee, couldn't resist. "Well, well, isn't this just like one of those old radio mysteries?"

Brandon, ignoring the quip, turned to me. "You said there was a notebook as well?"

"Yes!" I eagerly grabbed it and showed him some of the vital pages, along with the ledger in the back. "I found one of his paychecks in his file, with a paper that said 'dead words'. It had that amount on it." I pointed to the last payout.

"Who do you think put it there?"

"I'm not sure. Maybe someone else was catching on to the fraud that Gary was doing."

He nodded, flipping through it. "I'd like to tell you good job, but this was not a good job. You have to leave this to us."

"I know. Trust me, I've learned my lesson. I'll never do anything like this again."

Aunt Mattie snorted, but when we looked over to her, she only blinked innocently. "Allergies," she explained.

You'd think I'd feel relief at having this all out in the air, but there was another thing I had to confess. My stupidity. "There's something more," I said softly.

He groaned. "What's that?"

I explained how I tried to flush the guy out with my article and email. And how I made a plan to meet me at the coffee shop.

"Emily! How could you do that?" Brandon's voice was frustrated.

"Well, I wasn't going to meet him really," I said in defense. "I was going to sit across the street and get pictures. Proof that it was him."

"Yeah, because bad guys would never think you'd do that," he retorted, his tone a mix of sarcasm and genuine worry, reminding me of the dangers of playing with fire, especially when the flames could burn more than just evidence.

"I've messed up in a lot of ways. But stumbling across a murdered body kind of addles the common sense. At least for me."

"I'll say," Aunt Mattie retorted.

I ignored her. After all, she was the one who went through his wallet and got pictures. "Do we still meet him, or do you have enough evidence now to arrest him?

"You put us in a predicament tipping our hand. I can't emphasize enough how dangerous it was." he admonished.

"I know. I'm sorry."

"Bananas! That's what I tell her," Aunt Mattie piped in.

Brandon looked over at her with a raised eyebrow. "From everything I've heard at the station about you, I'd say she learned from the best."

Chapter Twenty-Two

Of course, I didn't get to go to the Dutch Cup. But I did send Brandon a picture of Gary from the Whisker Treat's site, so he knew who to look for. And Brandon didn't leave me in suspense, wondering what happened. He let me know as soon as it was all finished.

I heard Gary arrived at coffee shop, punctual as if he had no reason to suspect a trap. He wore a nondescript grey jacket, and still had his crutch, so he was easily identified.

Brandon played the part of me, the email sender. As Gary neared the table, Brandon raised his hand and gave the code phrase, "Dead Words."

He said, judging from Gary's facial expression, he did not like that. As Gary approached the table, a plain clothes man intercepted him to bring him outside. Gary tried to bolt, but with his gimpy leg, it was more of a comedy than anything. However, it was during the pat-down that the police found yet another needle on him, with enough drugs in it to kill fifteen men. One he had planned to use on me.

I listened to Brandon recount the story over the phone with a mixture of relief and triumph. The evidence I had gathered, the articles, the messages, all of it was now in the hands of the police, backed by witness testimony.

Of course, the new accountants at Whisker Treats quickly discovered the fraudulent activities that had been taking place. As they delved into the financial records, discrepancies became evident, revealing a pattern of deceit. The overwhelming evidence, including the notebook, transactions, and cassette tape, must have broke Gary, because he confessed right away. I heard he hoped to cut a plea deal.

Daniel and David's sister and mom were so grateful to have closure. I lucked out in a big way because David's sister inherited his estate and gave me post permission for going through the security box. I learned my lesson on this one. I was ready to hang up my detective hat for good.

The evening had settled over the my apartment like a big quilt of stars. I let out a sigh of relief that could've powered a small wind turbine, now that Gary was safely tucked away in custody.

Aunt Mattie had spent the day with me, ostensibly to get the news, but I think she needed company for her nerves as well. She'd made a huge pan of lasagna, something I'd loved from childhood, and even baked cookies. She even brought over Al Cabone, her dog, who'd joined Shakespeare for a serious case of the zoomies. The two animals now slept in a pile they'd made out of my bathrobe.

My aunt fluffed up the chair cushion like she was prepping for a pillow fight, before putting in a way to support her back. "Well, Emily, we did it," she announced. "I'm too old for this stuff." She adjusted her rhinestone glasses, the chain twinkling like a disco ball.

I poured the water into the teapot, the chamomile scent wafting through the air. "We did do it. Though, I hope this is my last gig as an amateur sleuth. I'd rather stick to blogging about cats than dodging bullets."

Aunt Mattie chuckled, taking her tea with a grateful nod. "Oh, my dear, where's the fun in that? Life's a stage, and sometimes we're the lead in a thriller we didn't audition for. Today, we were the blockbuster, if I do say so myself."

We sat in silence for a bit, sipping our tea, each lost in our thoughts. "I wonder if Brandon will ever want to talk to me again," I mused.

Aunt Mattie, ever the philosopher, fiddled with her kaleidoscope. "Of course, he will. Why he won his entire precinct's respect, I tell you that. And not just for solving these crimes. But for dealing with us so well. You know I have a reputation there." She grinned evilly.

"You like causing trouble, don't you?"

She sighed and shrugged. "It's a gift. Keeps life from being boring."

That's true. It's never boring around you."

"You know," she said, peering through the kaleidoscope. "Life is like this kaleidoscope. You think you're seeing one pattern, but give it a twist, and bam, new world. Our personalities are our twists."

I grinned. "I could do with some less vibrant days, Aunt Mattie."

Just then, the buzzer went off. It was Brandon, asking to come up. I buzzed him in, then heard his footsteps pounding up the stair. I had the door open by the time he hit the landing.

He came up with an enormous wild-flower bouquet in hand. "I know it's late, but figured we should celebrate, off the record, of course."

"That's so sweet! Come in, Brandon. I've got some left over lasagna, if you want some."

Brandon's eyes lit up. "Sounds great!"

As he stepped inside, Aunt Mattie winked at me, twirling her kaleidoscope in hand.

Afterword

Thank you for reading! I'm excited to share a new series! Book one, The Route 66 Misfits, starring Clara Fitzwater from the Secret Library Cozy Mystery series!

The famed Clara Fitzwater is now is trading her stage lights for detective work. Traveling in her restore ancient Volkswagen van, adorned with sun-bleached daisies and peace signs, she's living life just the way she wanted.

Until, late one night, she gets an urgent call from her niece, Jane, who's not just been mugged but is also upstaging the local drama scene with her unexpected starring role as the prime suspect.

With Jane's future hanging by a thread thinner than the script she's writing in jail, Clara and her actor friend, Archie, dive

AFTERWORD

into the investigation. Archie, sit-com extraordinaire, is more used to delivering punchlines than solving crimes. But he brings his comedic timing to the case, much to Clara's chagrin. Together, they navigate through the mystery to find who framed Jane.

Will Clara's theatrical flair and Archie's knack for improvisation be enough to unravel this mystery? Or will their curtain call come too soon, leaving Jane to face the final act alone?

Made in the USA
Monee, IL
23 December 2024